PETE & FREMONT

Jenny Tripp

PETE & FREMONT

With illustrations by John Manders

HARCOURT, INC.

Orlando ★ Austin ★ New York ★ San Diego ★ Toronto ★ London

Requests for permission to make copies of any part of the
work should be submitted online at www.harcourt.com/contact
or mailed to the following address: Permissions Department,
Harcourt, Inc., 6277 Sea Harbor Drive, Orlando, Florida 32887-6777.

www.HarcourtBooks.com

Library of Congress Cataloging-in-Publication Data
Tripp, Jenny.
Pete and Fremont/Jenny Tripp; illustrated by John Manders.
p. cm.
Summary: When circus owner Mike decides Pete the poodle has grown
too old to continue as the starring act, Pete forms an unlikely alliance
with a young grizzly bear, who only wants to go home to the woods.
[1. Circus animals—Fiction.   2. Poodles—Fiction.   3. Grizzly bear—Fiction.
4. Circus—Fiction.]   I. Manders, John, ill.   II. Title.
PZ7.T73572Pet   2007
[Fic]—dc22   2006008757
ISBN 978-0-15-205629-2

Text set in New Aster
Designed by April Ward

First edition
A C E G H F D B

Printed in the United States of America

For my dear papa,
who taught me to fly without a net,
and who never let me fall.

—J. T.

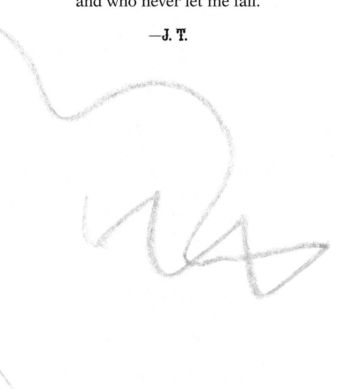

*   ★   ☆   ★   *

Life is being on the wire,
everything else is just waiting.

—*Karl Wallenda,*
lifelong aerialist and founder
of the Flying Wallendas

presenting
~ the ~ AMAZING,
~ the ~ MAGNIFICENT...
Me!

Call me Pete. Or my stage name, Pierre Le Chien. Even "Here, boy!" I answer to 'em all. On most days, a whistle will work, too. You do know how to whistle, don't you?

But if you call me Powder Puff, I just might take a piece out of your pants.

I was born in the sawdust of the center ring during a sold-out matinee on the hottest day of an Illinois

July. Mom, trouper that she was, went right ahead and finished her act, then tenderly laid me at the ringmaster's feet. The crowd went bananas.

The first smells my baby nose sniffed were greasepaint, elephant poop, and pink popcorn. The first sound in my baby ears was the thunder of a thousand hands clapping. To me, it's still the sweetest music there is.

Yeah, I'm circus, 101 percent. Circus folk are a tight little tribe. We have to be. We work together, eat together, travel together nine months of the year. Our bedrooms are railroad cars. Our schoolroom's a canvas tent. We've got our own language, our own superstitions, and our own way of looking at things.

My outfit, Circus Martinez, isn't the biggest show on earth by a long shot. Take our lion, Lucky. He's about as wild as your typical church bingo night. The closest he ever came to attacking anybody was when he dozed off with the trainer's head in his mouth. And our tiger, Zamba, the scary guy snarling on our poster? He ought to have a sign on his cage: WILL ROAR FOR FOOD.

Our props are on the mangy side. We've got one ring, not three. Some of our performers are a little long in the tooth. In fact, a couple I could name don't have any teeth at all. When the big top goes up, it's us performers who wrestle the ropes and drive the pegs. The lady who does the riding act moonlights sewing the costumes. And when he's not tying himself in knots, you'll find our contortionist working the ticket booth.

We mostly hit the smaller towns that the big shows miss—all those dusty little dots on the map between Here and There. But we give 'em plenty of marvel for their money. Old and young gasp, laugh, and clap themselves silly.

I've never known any other kind of life and never wanted to. Who would?

Oh, yeah. Did I mention I'm a poodle? Purebred Royal Standard. A nifty razzle-dazzle pink, as long as my trainer keeps my roots touched up. I'm top dog in Monsieur Moliere's Performing Pups. You've heard of us?

There are five of us dogs altogether. Me and Bob are the poodles. Scrappy's the cute little mixed breed with one floppy ear. Arthur's an Irish wolfhound, and he's as big as a baby buffalo. Then there's Lolly, better

known as The Pup. Lolly does all the cutesy bits, like
the baby carriage act with the clowns. Little kids and
old ladies go nuts for Lolly.

But they save the big applause for me. They know
star quality when they see it.

Dancing on your hind legs probably doesn't sound
like much of a trick to a human. But try doing it on a
five-foot rolla-bolla ball, twirling a tasseled baton in
your teeth at the same time.

And how about this for a knock-'em-dead finale?

The drumroll starts, then the spotlight hits me. My
spangled jacket shimmers like a bucket full of stars.
I take a flying leap off the springboard and throw
in a double midair flip. Then I sail dive through
the flaming hoop and—*splash!*—
into the kiddy pool.

That, my friend, is
show biz.

That's what makes me a headliner, while Lolly is stuck in the baby buggy with a big pink pacifier in her muzzle. Was it my fault she dreamed of knocking me out of the star spot? Or plotted shady schemes to ease me out of the act?

She might have got her way, too—if Fremont hadn't shown up when he did.

But I'm getting ahead of myself. I guess the very best place to begin is with the very worst day of my life.

CHAPTER 1

Saturday, June 12, a year ago this summer, is a day I'll never forget. And believe me, I've tried. We were playing a woodsy little town, up near the top of the map. The evening show was sold out as usual.

I lost my puppy teeth long ago, but I'm all the dog I ever was—or most of it, anyway. But on this particular evening, there was a kind of rainy fog hanging around that seemed to sink into my bones.

My hind legs were stiff. I could feel a little twinge in my walk that worried me. I first noticed it at rehearsal, when I blew my somersault coming off the rolla-bolla ball.

Sophie, Imelda, and Czarina—the Lipizzaner sisters—were getting their glossy, white manes braided in the wings and saw me go sprawling in the sawdust. "Peter, you are all right?" Sophie whinnied, tossing her long, elegant head.

The Lipizzaner mares are what you'd call circus royalty. Their ancestors played the Colosseum back in ancient Rome, and they don't let anyone forget it. But there's no harder working horses in show business, or nags with more heart. They'd go on with three broken legs if they had to.

"Nah, Sophie, just missed my mark," I barked back, as Mike, our trainer, bent down to pat me.

"Hurt yourself, old boy?" Mike asked softly, checking my back legs with careful, sure hands. The "old boy" hurt worse than the fall, but I licked his face anyhow, just to let him know I was okay. He and his wife, Greta, are pretty bright, as people go. But when you're trying to communicate with humans, you've got to keep it simple.

Wouldn't you know it, Lolly was right there, too. She batted puppy-dog eyes back at me from under her bonnet. "Hope you're not too shook to do the finale," she cooed.

"Don't get your hopes up," I snapped.

She was practically drooling to hear that I wouldn't be going on. Fat chance! I gave her a toothy smile, then jumped up and did a flip, just to show her. I wasn't about to let this upstart mutt think I was gonna play dead while she bumped me out of the spotlight.

"Bravo, Bone Breath!" I heard Rita holler from the high wire, where she was lazing around as usual. "But you better save it for show time. Who knows how many more of those you got in you?"

She wouldn't have made that crack if she'd been

down here where I could get to her. But that's a chimp for you. Just smart enough to keep out of snapping distance but too dumb to keep her trap shut.

I've known Rita all my life, but she's not gonna win "most popular" any time soon. Opposable thumbs and a twisted sense of humor make a rotten combination. Who else would—or even could?—pull the kind of practical jokes Rita does? Like when she stuck a lollipop on PeeWee the ostrich's tail feathers? The poor dope started whirling so fast trying to catch hold of that sucker, he plowed smack into the cotton candy machine. Neither of them has really been the same since.

Anyhow, I've discovered that the best way to deal with a smart aleck like Rita is to let what she says just blow by me. So I went on with rehearsal and didn't muff it again.

But I knew she and Lolly would be watching tonight.

*　*　☆　*　*

The first fifteen minutes of a show are my favorite part. The band starts to play. The crowd presses though the ticket gates and climbs into the bleachers.

The big top is stretched tight overhead, striped bright red and white like a colossal peppermint drop. Little kids are clutching their balloons and cotton candy, so excited they can't sit still.

Backstage, everyone's zipping up costumes and daubing on greasepaint, checking props and warming up. The air is buzzing with the feeling that something amazing could happen, will happen, any minute now.

Then the horns blare a fanfare, and the spotlight hits the ringmaster center ring. Lifting his top hat, he bellows, "Ladies and gentlemen, boys and girls, welcome to the Biggest Little Circus on Earth—*Circus Martinez!*"

His big black whip hisses and cracks—S-s-s-s-s-s-snap!—as the band swings into our theme song. Places, everyone! It's magic time.

Tonight, like all those other nights, us dogs and our humans were ready and waiting in the wings. Scrappy, his clown hat in place, was chewing at his stubby tail, trying to squash a frisky flea. Lolly, baby bonnet tied under her chin, was sprawled on the floor, probably daydreaming about spitting her pacifier out for good. Mike's wife, Greta, was giving my pom-pom a final fluff.

Scraps laid off his tail and cocked his head at me. "That was a rough tumble you took, Pete. You all right?" he asked.

I could see Lolly's ears perk up.

"Never better, Scraps," I answered, but I was looking at Lolly when I said it.

I could see the other dogs trading worried looks. Nobody likes bad feeling in the act. But there was no time to pick that bone now. Up on hind legs, we jogged briskly out from the wings, me in the lead and Mike and Greta bringing up the rear. On with the show!

When you're doing a performance, time seems to go by in a flash, like someone's pushed the fast-forward button. Ba-da-bing, ba-da-boom, ba-da-bam! The next thing I know I'm twirling my baton and making the rolla-bolla ball sail circles around the ring. The crowd's loving me, and I'm loving them back. The twinge in my hindquarters is history.

I dash smartly into place on the end of the springboard for the finale. I can feel Lolly's greedy gaze on me. Let her look, I think to myself, and see how a real star shines!

The drumroll begins, deep and exciting, and the spotlight hits my spangled jacket. Greta quickly rolls the kiddy pool into place. Mike sets the hoop on the stand and lights it on fire.

The crowd holds its breath. Even the littlest kids stop hollering and hold still. All eyes are on me. The trumpet sounds my cue. I give a mighty leap, and the springboard throws me high into the air. One flip, two flips, three—

And that's when it all goes up in smoke.

Literally.

CHAPTER 2

Yeeeaoowww! When I flew through the flaming hoop, my big, beautiful pink pom-pom tail caught fire! I missed the kiddy pool entirely and hit the ground running.

I bet you're thinking, why didn't he just jump into the pool and put it out? Maybe everyone would have thought it was part of the act? But it's a funny thing having your tail on fire. It seems to drive whatever sense you've got clean out of your head. So instead of doing the smart thing, I was ripping laps around the ring and howling like a fire truck.

Mass hysteria! Every kid in the bleachers was squalling at the top of his lungs. Greta got so rattled she fell into the pool. Poor Mike was chasing me. And

to make matters worse, the band suddenly struck up "Waltz of the Flowers," the cue for the Lipizzaner sisters to come galloping out!

Then one of the clowns aimed a bucket of water at me and hit Sophie by mistake. Her towering feathered headdress flopped over her eyes. She lost her step and nearly dragged her sisters down on top of her!

Just about that time I got my brains back and
hopped into the kiddy pool with Greta. A long, steamy
hiss rose from my roasted rump.

It took the ringmaster and the whole clown troop
to get things back in order. Us dogs beat a panicked,
pell-mell retreat to the wings.

I wasn't hurt much—at least not on the outside.

True, my tail was but a blackened remnant of its former puffy pink perfection. But my pride was what had really gone up in smoke.

What a comedown! What a disaster! In all my years in show business, this was the bottom—in every sense of the word.

I huddled in the cool grass under the wheels of the lion cage. Nursing my sore tail, I snapped at any animal dumb enough to get close. The last thing I wanted was sympathy.

When Mike came to rub a little soothing ointment on my unhappy ending, I crawled out of hiding and licked his hand. It was all the apology I could muster.

Bless his heart, he wasn't mad. In fact, he was extra gentle putting on that goose grease.

But his words were daggers to my doggy heart.

"Poor old Pete," he sighed.

Old? I didn't like the sound of that.

"I should have taken you out of the headline spot a long time ago," he said. "It's just not fair to push you so hard at your age."

What?! Give up my spot? Was he kidding?

This kind of talk had to be nipped in the bud—and pronto. Ignoring my broiled behind, I popped up as pert as a pup and started throwing flips. I didn't care if I churned myself into butter. I was gonna show him I was still the star!

He just laughed and clapped.

When I stopped to catch my breath, Mike ruffled the pom-pom on my head. "Good ol' Pete. Always ready to work, aren't you, boy?"

"Yarf!" I yipped. He chuckled, then got up and knocked the dirt off his knees.

"You're a trouper, Pete. And maybe you still got it in you to be top dog. But the good of the act comes first. The show must go on, right? I'll give you one more chance, but if you can't handle the hoop jump . . ." He shook his head. "Well, we'll cross that bridge when we come to it, eh? And let's hope we never do."

"Yarf!" I agreed. And I meant it.

The show would go on, and with me in it.

That performance was our last in that particular town. We loaded up our railroad cars that night and left while the village slept.

Us animals got cozy in our stalls, cages, and kennels. I hit my basket and was preparing to grab some shut-eye when PeeWee the ostrich popped his big goofy head over the partition between our rooms. He goggled at me, almost bursting with news.

PeeWee's what we call our circus telephone. Whatever goes into those little ears of his runs right out his big beak—maybe because there's no brain in the way to slow it down.

"Guess what, Pete?" he began.

I wasn't in the mood to play. "My tail's feeling much better; thanks for asking," I replied, digging at an imaginary flea.

PeeWee blinked, tilting his little head to the side in confusion. Then he barreled on. "Did you hear the news about Lolly?"

"What about her?" The words were out of my muzzle before I could stop myself.

"Well! Lolly's training to take your act with the springboard. Mike's been rehearsing her, and he told Greta that she's a natural. He said it was just like she'd been practicing on her own! In fact, he said—"

"Is this a private funeral or can anyone join the party?"

Oh, great. The last animal I wanted to see—Rita. She'd hoisted herself up onto the ledge next to Pee-Wee's head. She grinned down at me, her ugly little legs swinging.

PeeWee eyed her suspiciously and scooted away quickly. He'd never really forgiven her for that incident with the cotton candy machine.

"What's the matter, Feather Duster? Get your neck in a knot?" she taunted, reaching out to tweak his

beak. PeeWee jerked his head back so fast he banged it against the wall. Rita cackled, then turned to me. Her eyes twinkled with evil glee.

"So it's Clown Alley for you, eh, Pete?" she sneered.

"Maybe if you're real good, they'll let you ride in the baby carriage."

I gave her a grin that showed all of my teeth. "Don't be silly. Mike's just teaching Lolly the act in case I pull a muscle or something. Which I won't."

Rita shook her head. I thought I could see something that looked like pity in her homely face. "Face it, Pete. Tonight was your swan song. Isn't it better to go gracefully? Maybe even help Lolly learn the act? Show the world you're the bigger dog."

"Sorry to disappoint you, Rita, but PeeWee's got it all wrong, as usual. I'm a long, long way from finished. So if you're thinking of throwing me a bone voyage party—"

Rita snorted. "A long way from finished? Ha! Buddy, in dog years, you're dead!"

Her big mistake was thinking that my sore tail would slow me down. It didn't.

Before she could scramble to safety, I flew through the air and snapped a piece out of her hairy shin. Rita let out a shriek that got the big cats roaring two cars down.

"I hope when the clowns finish with you, they have you stuffed!" she yelled as she limped off to her own car. PeeWee, who'd ducked down during the ruckus, bobbed up again.

"Maybe you'd like to be alone?" he asked. A growl sent him galloping off. Alone is exactly what I wanted to be. I knew I could count on PeeWee to spread that around. My brain was buzzing like a beehive. Could Pee-Wee be right? Was Mike really giving me the heave-ho? No, he'd promised me one more chance!

Hadn't he?

With a head full of worries, my cozy old pillow felt like a bagful of rocks. No matter how many times I trotted around my basket, I just couldn't seem to get comfortable.

The clickety-clack of the rolling wheels was usually as soothing as a lullaby. But tonight, they seemed to be singing, "All washed up, all washed up . . ."

I don't know how long I'd been asleep when the squeal of the brakes woke me up. A bolt of lightning cut through the black sky beyond my window, followed by a drumroll of thunder that set my teeth on edge. Outside, I could hear men shouting and the clash of chains. Why had we stopped? Had the train broken down?

Then, louder than all of it, even drowning out the thunder, came a roar the likes of which I'd never heard before.

Something big let out that roar. Not a lion or a tiger. Bigger. Much bigger. The sound made the fur on my back stand up, and it was all I could do not to whimper.

There was a pile of boxes stacked against the wall. I scrambled up onto them and peeked out the little barred window, half curious and half scared of what I might see.

What I saw was a monster.

CHAPTER 4

It stood fifteen feet tall, with thick black fur that was slick with rain. Its arms were as big around as a man's middle. Its head was the size of a barrel. But no barrel ever had teeth like that—a set of choppers that made our lion's mighty mouthful look like baby teeth.

Seven men were fighting to hold the beast on ropes. One of them was our wild-animal trainer, Boston Charlie.

Boston Charlie struts around in his safari suit like he's all that and a bag of popcorn. He's got a nifty little pistol that he's never fired and a hairpiece that looks like roadkill. He keeps our two big cats—Lucky, the

lion, and Zamba, our tiger—hopping, but that's a lot less dangerous than it looks.

Zamba's in it strictly for the chow. That tiger never thinks of anything but his stomach. As long as he knows there's a juicy piece of meat waiting, he'll sing Italian opera if Charlie tells him to. And Lucky? It's all he can do to stay awake. I've seen rugs that were livelier.

But this was no tame kitty cat. For once, Boston Charlie wasn't looking so sure of himself. He and the ringmaster were crowded up against the train in their rain slickers, trying to stay out of the reach of the massive paws.

"I don't know, Chief," I heard Charlie shout to the ringmaster. "This thing's a little out of my league."

"You're a wild-animal trainer, ain't you?" the ringmaster snapped.

"Yeah, but not this wild," Charlie whined. "I already got an act—"

"You got a lion with a comb-over and a tiger that belongs in a petting zoo! How much longer will people pay to see them? If this show don't get a new attraction pretty soon, we're all gonna starve."

"I'd sooner starve than get eaten," Charlie muttered, but the ringmaster was already walking away.

Just then, a guy jumped up behind the monster and jabbed it with something. A moment later, the thing hit the ground like dropped laundry. It took all seven men to drag it onto the train.

A few minutes later, the train wheels began to roll again. We were on our way like nothing had happened. I wondered for a moment if the whole thing hadn't been a bad dream. Surely, nothing could be as big as that. . . .

A sudden hiss from the top of my kennel made me look up. There, to my surprise, was Rita. I noticed she was being extra careful to keep her digits out of snapping distance.

"What do you want, Bananas-for-brains?" I barked. I'd had enough of Rita for one night.

"Did you see what I just saw?" she whispered, jerking a thumb toward the window. "Oh, and I forgive you for trying to bite me, Bone Breath."

"What do you mean, 'trying'?" I yipped.

Ignoring my question, she asked, "What did you make of that thing outside? What kind of an animal did it look like to you?"

I cocked my head to one side. "A gorilla, maybe?"

Rita shook her head. "Where could they trap a gorilla out here in the sticks?"

"Trap? You mean that thing's wild?" I gasped. Wild ain't natural, not in the circus. Like I told you, we're all pros here. Wild? Wild is strictly amateur hour.

"What did you think, genius? The big guy just got up on the wrong side of the bed?" She leaned down, grinning that wicked grin. "What say you and me go welcome our new member?"

I thought of the monster and the way he'd flung grown men around like rag dolls. Maybe I didn't want to get any closer to him than I already was.

Rita seemed to read my thoughts.

"Come on, Pete! He's just a fellow animal. One of us, right? Hey, you're not scared, are you?" Without waiting for my answer, she lifted the latch on my kennel door and swung it wide open. "After you, Le Chien."

I wasn't about to act chicken in front of a chimp. So I led the way down the dark corridor. Rita loped close behind me.

The animal cars rocked gently as the train rolled along. I could hear soft snores and snorts coming from behind bars and doors. The air was sleepy and still, lush with the scents of hay, horse, and big cat.

"Where you guys goin'?" honked an anxious voice. Rita and I both jumped a foot, then tried to pretend we hadn't. PeeWee was gawking down at us from his stall. "Why'd we stop? What was all that noise outside? Who . . ."

"What is this, twenty questions?" Rita snapped, pulling me along.

"Can I come?" PeeWee hollered after us.

As we got closer to the baggage car where they'd stowed our mystery guest, I kept waiting for a human to show up and stop us.

Nobody did.

The big sliding door was latched closed. From inside, I could hear the shuffle of heavy footsteps and the clank of iron. Whatever they'd poked him with was wearing off fast.

"Let me climb up on your back, Pete," Rita whispered, then jumped on me before I could think of a good reason why she shouldn't. She grabbed the door handle and twisted it with all her strength. The darn thing slid open as easy as you please. Rita hopped down, and we both peered into the gloom beyond. Darker than the darkness around him, we could see his lumpy outline at the far end of the car.

And he could see us, too. The footsteps stopped.

"You talk to him, Pete," Rita said. "He's a paw walker like you."

I edged forward about half an inch and cleared my

throat. "Uh, welcome aboard. I take it you're joining our little troupe?"

No answer, just heavy breathing.

"My name's Pete. What's yours?" I tried.

Still nothing. Definitely the strong, silent type. "We could come back when you're settled in—"

Suddenly, Rita gave me a shove in the rump that sent me stumbling forward. The Thing reared up to its full height just as lightning ripped open the sky outside. He roared so loud I could feel his hot breath on my muzzle. The swipe of a paw the size of a tennis racquet tickled the fur on my neck.

With a yip of terror I turned tail and ran all the way back to my kennel, Rita right on my heels. When we were finally home free, I panted, "What were you trying to do, feed me to him?"

Rita wasn't even listen-
ing. "Did you see
the size of him?"
she asked, eyes
wide. "I've never
seen one half that
big before!"

"One what?" I demanded.

Rita cocked her head in surprise. "Good grief, Pete. Don't you know a grizzly bear when you see one?!"

A bear? I'd seen bears, of course. There was a troop of Russian bears we used to travel with. They danced and juggled. One of them rode a little bicycle.

Somehow I couldn't picture the monster in the baggage car tootling around the ring on a two-wheeler any time soon.

Rita got an evil gleam in her eye, then she burst into shrieks of laughter, rolling on the floor and grabbing her toes. "Our new attraction, huh? Oh, baby! I can't wait to see Boston Charlie shake a chair at that ol' boy and tell him to roll over! Gonna be a whole new ball game!"

I laughed right along with her, mostly because I was glad to be alive and in one piece. Of course, if either of us had known how right Rita was, we wouldn't have been laughing.

We'd have been looking for a place to hide.

CHAPTER 5

The rest of our troupe got their first look at the bear the next day. We'd just set up camp, and most of us were in the tent warming up.

The cats were waiting in their cage in the middle of the ring. Zamba the tiger was pacing back and forth, working up an appetite. Lucky the lion was paws-up

on the floor taking a catnap. Puffs of sawdust rose up with every snore. Senora Paloma, the lady who runs the bird act, was turning her trained pigeons into doves with talcum powder. Czarina and Imelda were chewing the cud as their sister Sophie worked on a new dance step with Madame Suzette, their trainer. Show business as usual.

To my relief, Mike didn't say a word about taking me out of the headline spot. I trotted to my mark, took my jump, and even threw in a twist or two on my flips. I sailed through the center of the hoop as clean as one of Robin Hood's arrows.

"Attaboy, Pete!" Mike said, tossing me a treat. I gulped it down, glad to see that things were back to normal. If Lolly still had any boneheaded ideas about taking my job, she could drag 'em out and bury 'em in the backyard.

In fact, I was just about to tell her so when a commotion sprung up that made every one of us—animal and human—stop in our tracks.

It was the Monster. He was weighted down with so much iron it looked as if he could barely move. Boston Charlie was right behind him, poking him with a chair. Charlie was trying to look cool, like he did this

kind of thing every day. But I noticed that he was stay-
ing as far out of reach as he could. And he had his pistol stuck in his belt where he could grab it in a hurry.

Last night the bear had looked black, but dried out
and in the daylight he was reddish brown, like a cin-
namon stick. He still looked big, though. Super sized,
even for a grizzly.

"Mercy!" Sophie Lipizzaner skidded to a stop that
nearly sent poor Madame flying over her head. "Vhere
in ze vherld did zat come from?"

I would have filled her in, but something told me
I'd better keep my eyes on our furry Frankenstein if I
valued my curly pink hide.

Rita came loping up. "Looks like Charlie's finally
got a chance to try out his pop gun!"

Maybe the grizzly heard her. Or maybe he'd just
caught sight of the big-cat cage. Because when the
gate rattled open in front of him, the bear raised up
and bellowed so loud that the bars shook. And they
weren't the only ones. Zamba backed away so fast that
his striped hindquarters hit the bars on the far side.

Boston Charlie dropped the chair and grabbed for
his gun. But the griz sent it spinning through the air
with one swipe of his paw. Cornered, Charlie grabbed

the center pole of the tent and started up. He was climbing faster than I'd ever seen a human go, yelling for help the whole way. And the bear was going after him!

Paloma's pigeons took off in a flutter. Sophie gave an ear-splitting whinny, and she and her sisters went galloping out of the ring in a ministampede. Lolly, Scrappy, and the rest of my act whizzed by me so fast I could feel a breeze.

I knew I should run, but it was like my paws were glued to the floor. Rita must have had the same problem, because she was right beside me.

Above us, Charlie was straining to grab a trapeze bar hanging just beyond his reach. It looked for a moment like he might be able to catch hold of it and swing to safety. But the bear wrapped those tree trunk arms of his around the tent pole and shook it, just like you'd shake a peach tree to get the fruit to fall. The canvas overhead flapped and snapped like a whip. Charlie had to hang on for dear life. Now he was really hollering.

Just then, the griz glanced over his shoulder and looked me straight in the eye. It was just a glance—but I read him like a human reads a book.

"He's scared, Rita," I breathed, hardly believing it myself.

"No kidding, Bone Breath," Rita cackled nervously. "It's gonna take two men and a crowbar to pry Charlie off that pole."

"No, not Charlie!" I said. "The bear! The bear is scared of Charlie. Of all of us!"

Boom! Something went off like a firecracker behind me. The bear shuddered, then let go of the pole. He crumpled to the ground in a big, hairy heap. I looked back and saw the ringmaster standing in the doorway in his underwear and socks. He was clutching the tranquilizer gun and shaking like he had the chills. All at once, it was quiet.

Lucky, who hadn't moved a muscle until then, lifted his head and gave his mane a shake.

"Hey, keep it down, you guys," he growled, blinking and yawning. "Can't a cat catch a nap around here?"

CHAPTER 6

You can guess what the main topic of conversation was at feeding time that afternoon.

Sophie Lipizzaner was the first to speak up. "Vhat in the vherld vas za ringmaster zhinking when he brought in zat—zat amateur? Are ve running circus or zoo?!" Her sisters, mouths full of oats, nodded in agreement.

Zamba shook his big, striped head, mystified. "Can you imagine being nuts enough to try and bite the hand that feeds you?!"

"For once I agree with you," Rita chimed in, peeling a banana with her nimble toes. "The sooner Boston Charlie and the ringmaster get rid of that walking disaster area, the safer we'll be. He's a menace!"

I still don't know what got into me. I mean, it wasn't like the bear had greeted me with open arms— more like open jaws. But something made me want to stick up for him. Maybe it was the fear I'd seen in his eyes. Or the way he'd fought back in spite of it.

"Ah, come on. Give the big guy a break!" I said. "It's not his fault he's new to the game. Everybody's got to start somewhere!"

Sophie tossed her mane and peered down her long nose at me. "Zhere is no room under za big top for an animal zat doesn't know his business, Pete. Za sooner he's back in vhatever vilderness he came from, za better for him and for za circus."

The rest of them growled, chirped, or neighed their agreement. PeeWee batted his eyes and said, "I heard the ringmaster tell Boston Charlie he's got two weeks to teach the bear some manners. Otherwise, he's gonna get rid of him."

"Two weeks? Why so long?" Rita chuckled, tossing the banana peel into the trash barrel. "Only took the bear two seconds to teach Charlie how to climb a pole."

Lucky, awake for once, lazily scratched his back against the side of his cage. "Nobody's gonna teach that big dummy anything. These wild types can't even speak the language. I say give him a one-way ticket home and good riddance. Animals like that make us all look bad."

I shrugged and went back to the nice meaty bone that Mike had given me. After all, what was the bear to me, or me to the bear? We weren't even the same species. And I knew that Sophie was right about one thing. The big top is no place for rookies.

In fact, it ain't always that peachy a place for pros.

CHAPTER 7

In art, just like in life, nerve and timing are everything. One without the other? Disaster, or worse. Look at Romeo and Juliet. Plenty of nerve, but lousy timing, and what did it get them? Starring roles but unhappy endings. Nerve plus timing equals glory. Nerve without timing? Tragedy.

So it was with me, Pierre Le Chien. Tragedy caught up with me in a town so small you probably never heard of it unless you were born there. The name doesn't matter. To tell you the truth, it's even slipped my needle-sharp mind. Let's just call it . . . Pits Burg.

They don't get much in the way of traveling entertainment in Pits Burg, so the whole town had turned out to catch Circus Martinez. The audience was loving us, and no wonder. We were stupendous.

Especially me.

I'd made a major effort to put all thoughts of my burned tail behind me. Tonight was my chance to show Mike that I still had what it took to be top dog. And I gave it everything I had.

I bounced from one stunt to the next like I was made out of rubber. I whipped that ol' rolla-bolla ball around the ring so fast, it smoked. I had the audience eating out of my paw. I knew it and so did Mike. So much for putting me out to pasture! It was the greatest performance of my career—right up to the finale.

Right up to the lousy, stinking flaming hoop.

The guy who invented that sizzling showstopper should have to spend the rest of his life jumping through one. That would be justice. But I wasn't thinking about justice this fateful night in Pits Burg. I was thinking about "one more chance," then I hit my springboard and went twisting through the air.

I can't say where it happened exactly. Somewhere between the springboard and the hoop a picture popped into my mind. Just a picture—of me flying through the air, only with my tail flaring like some kind of furry Roman candle. It was as if I was watching the whole thing from the bleachers, along with the pop-eyed audience.

In that instant, doubt sank its fangs into me like a rabid dog. Whoosh! There went my timing and my nerve, up in smoke faster than a short fuse.

Oh, the horror! I missed my jump entirely, skimming under the hoop and sprawling into the sawdust!

Before I could scramble to my feet, I saw Lolly shoot out of the baby carriage, spitting out her pacifier as she went. To our amazement, and the audience's delight, she leaped off the springboard and sung through that hoop like she'd been doing it all her life. She hit the kiddy pool with a splash, then sprung out panting with excitement. Her tail was waving like a soggy victory banner.

Flat on my back in the sawdust, I closed my eyes. If wishing you were dead could actually kill you, they never would have opened again.

The crowd was on its feet, barking like a herd of seals. Lolly just kept turning and turning, begging for more.

The band struck up our exit music, and I could see the Lipizzaner sisters waiting in the wings. I got up and trailed off after my troupe.

Mike was hugging Lolly like a madman, and she was licking his face. "You wonderful, wonderful pooch!" he cried, practically weeping with gratitude. "You saved the day!"

The other dogs crowded around them, adding their two cents' worth of little yips and yaps of praise.

"Smooth move, Lolly!"

"You go, dog!"

But they all shut up and stepped back as I approached. Mike set Lolly down.

"Well, Pete. Good thing Lolly jumped in when she did, eh?"

I could feel the other dogs watching me, waiting.

I'm proud to say that I stood tall and did the right thing. "Nice work, Lolly. You saved the show," I mumbled, then slunk away. What it cost me, only I and the Big Dog Upstairs will ever know.

Mike followed me outside. He crouched down and fed me a doggie treat. My favorite flavor, too—bacon cheddar. Tonight it tasted more like a chunk of cardboard.

He let me have it without any beating around the bush. "Lolly's gonna take the springboard business from now on, pal."

Well, there it was. My nightmare come true. I had finally hit bottom. As miserable as I was at that moment, one thought cheered me up a little. Things couldn't possibly get worse.

Or could they?

Seeting the look in my eyes, Mike bent down and scratched me behind the ear.

"Don't look so sad, old fella. You're not out of the show—not by a long shot. In fact, I've got a brand new act for you!"

A new act? For me?! Now he was talkin'! My tail thumped the ground.

Mike saw it and grinned back at me. "That's right, Pete! It's an idea the clowns cooked up. It's gonna be a showstopper—the Canine Cannonball!"

It took all my self-control not to bite him.

Me, a star, reduced to—ammunition?!

Mike, no mind reader, took my heartbroken sob for

a yip of joy. "Yep, you take it easy from now on, old-timer. Let the young ones do the jumping around."

And he left. If dogs could cry, I'd have been bawling like a baby. I could see the paw print on the wall, and it wasn't pretty. I was sidelined, benched, KO'd clean out of the ring. What was I supposed to do? Sit around the Old Animals' Home in Florida slobbering over my scrapbook?

No, a thousand times no!

I had to come up with a brand new act—and fast. Or else that was the way the doggie biscuit was gonna crumble. It made my tail curl just to think about it. I stumbled off into the darkness of the empty fairgrounds.

I don't know how long I wandered. I do recall passing up a perfectly good chunk of pink popcorn—a treat I'd have walked over hot coals for any other time. And I might have roamed all night, if a rumbling growl hadn't stopped me cold.

My heart bumped in my chest. I'm about as deaf to my natural instincts as an animal can be. But now they were sounding off like a car alarm. I was about to become some bigger beast's late-night snack.

Trying to make myself look as small and unappetizing as possible, I began to creep backward. My keen doggie nose told me the menace was crouched just ahead of me, but where? It was so dark . . .

Then all at once, my eyes adjusted, and I could see who—or should I say what?—had growled that growl. In a shake, I stood up straight. The hair on my back lay down like it was supposed to. Me, scared? Not anymore.

See, it was none other than Mr. Big Mouth Bear, terror of the Circus Martinez. But this time, he was locked up nice and tight in an old lion cage. He didn't sound too happy about it. But I was fresh out of sympathy.

"Go ahead," I snarled, "Growl away, you big, hairy buzz saw. What do you know about trouble? Nothing! You, they gotta drag you in here kicking and squalling, and for what? To give you a free shot at the big time. To try and turn you into a star! Me? I spend my whole life working to be top dog. And the minute I show a little weakness, they toss me aside like yesterday's candy wrappers! You think you got trouble, Teddy? Try walking a mile on my paws! Try being the Canine Cannonball!"

A long silence followed, broken only by a ragged panting that I slowly realized was coming from me.

Just like that, all the fight went out of me. What was I doing? Carrying on like some kind of nut, yelping at a guy who might as well have been a brick wall. He couldn't understand me. I shook my head, disgusted—mostly with myself.

"Jeesh, why am I wasting my breath on you? Mike's right. I'm perfect for the cannonball." I turned away and started walking toward the lights of the tent.

A voice behind me froze me in my tracks. Not the kind of voice you'd expect. A big voice, sure—but a kid's voice. Cracking a little on the low notes, unsure of itself.

"What's a ca-ca-cannonball?" asked the bear.

CHAPTER 9

Amazed, **I whirled** to stare at the bear, who was staring back at me. It took me a moment to get my jaw working again. When I finally did, the best I could manage was a choked "You—you spoke? You speak?"

The bear sighed, "Well, duh."

I remembered our first meeting back in the railroad car and demanded, "Why didn't you say anything when I talked to you before?"

I waited for him to answer. His big head drooped. When he finally did, his voice sounded rough, like he was trying not to cry.

"Because I was scared! All those humans yelling and sticking me with stuff—putting me into that stinky

box and putting these—these—?" He paused, raising his arms to show me.

"Chains," I filled in.

"Chains on me. And you came in, with that ugly thing that looks like them—"

I snickered. "Rita. She's a chimp. But I see what you mean."

"—and you smelled like them, and I just thought—

well, I guess I didn't think. I was mad. I'm sorry if I scared you. Why are you that weird color?"

I blinked in surprise. "It's not weird, it's pink. And it's part of my costume."

"What's a costume?"

"A costume? Something a performer puts on, to dress up his act. To give it pizzazz!"

The bear looked baffled. "What's an act?"

The kid had a lot to learn. "An act? It's what we do," I explained. "We're in show biz, see? We entertain people."

The bear scowled, letting his head drop. "I hate people. I don't want to be a show biz."

I didn't bother to correct his grammar. "You don't know what you're talking about, kid. Show business is the greatest thing in the world! Three meals a day, and all the travel, the fans, the love a dog could want! It's heaven. Or as close as I'm gonna get."

"Then you like being a—a cannonball?"

Ouch. "I wasn't always a cannonball, kid. I was a headliner! And I will be again!" I snarled. I could see the bear draw back. I felt a little guilty. There was the big hair ball pouring out his heart to me. And here I was, snapping at him like a crotchety Scottie. "Where you from, pal?"

The bear sighed again, remembering. "The woods. The mountains."

I shuddered. "You mean—outside?"

"It's nice there," he said shyly. "It's quiet and it smells clean, like trees and sunshine. Not like this." He waved a super-sized paw at his cage.

"That's just lion smell. Big cat. You'll get used to it, kid. You'll get used to everything. Even humans—"

The bear's big face crumpled at that. He laid his face on his paws. I could barely hear him. "I don't want to get used to it! I want to go home!"

This last part came out more like a howl than a growl. My heart melted. How would I feel in his place, torn from my happy home? I tried to picture myself in the woods, alone with a bunch of trees, fresh air, and sunshine. Yikes! Enough to make a dog's blood run cold—this dog, anyhow.

It wasn't like my friends had given him a big circus welcome. He must have sensed how they felt about him. Maybe he even heard some of their catty comments. Weren't wild animals supposed to have super-sensitive hearing? Besides, it hadn't been his idea to run off and join the circus. He was nothing but a homesick kid.

Call me a softie—or a sucker. But before my good sense had time to speak, I pushed and squeezed myself between the bars of his cage. There I stood before him, just one four legger to another. The bear jerked his head up in surprise. His lips drew back, showing big, white teeth. I tried not to look.

"We both got troubles, I guess," I said. "But if you want a friend, you got one."

He blinked at me like he couldn't quite believe it. "For true?" he asked softly.

I nodded. "For true."

He hesitated a moment, suddenly shy again, then asked, "Would you stay here with me? There's noises and stuff, and I—I get scared."

Scared? Him? That was a laugh. "I guess I can stand it if you can," I agreed. Just like any kid when he gets his way, he brightened right up. I circled a spot, then lay down. The bear flopped beside me, sending up a dust cloud. We snuggled down in the sweet, dry hay.

I was just drifting off to dreamland when he murmured, "Hey. What's your name?"

"Pierre Le Chien. Call me Pete. What's yours?"

The bear gave a happy little sigh. "Fremont."

"Good night, Fremont." I yawned.

"Good night, Pete."

CHAPTER 10

I was still snoozing at dawn's early light, when a siren wail sent my eyelids flapping up like window shades. You'd think nobody'd have more than one scream like that in them, but Rita did. There she stood—or rather, bounced—screeching her head off. Fremont stirred, then growled.

"For heaven's sake, get a grip!" I yelped. "I'm not deaf! Though I will be if you keep that up."

Rita stopped bouncing. "He—he hasn't killed you!?"

I yawned and stretched. "Do I look dead to you?"

I could see Rita was about to give a smart-alecky answer. I didn't want Fremont to get the wrong idea— or the right one—about her, so I cut her off. "Rita, I want you to meet a new friend of mine. He was feeling a little shy the other night. This is Fremont. Fremont, this is Rita. Like I said, she's one of us."

Rita eyed Fremont, then me. "You're saying this thing can talk, Pete?"

"Of course he can talk—when he finds somebody worth talking to!" I snapped. "Go on, Fremont. Talk to Rita. Tell her what you think she looks like."

Her eyes snapped at that. "Yeah, Fremont," Rita dared him. "Go on and tell me." And we both turned to stare at the griz—

—who, instead of telling her, gave an ugly snuffling snort and turned his back on us.

Rita rocked on her butt, cackling with laughter.

"Talks, huh? Oh, sure he does. Probably sings show tunes, too, if you get him in the mood!" she sniggered.

I could feel my nose getting hot with embarrassment. "Fremont, say something!" I begged. "Anything! Show her, go on! Say, 'Hello, Rita!'"

Fremont's reply was to curl up into a lumpy heap and do his imitation of a boulder.

I couldn't believe it! If he hadn't stunk like an old gym sock, I'd have bitten his big bear behind.

"Good-bye, Pete." Rita was already loping off toward the tent.

I sent Fremont a dirty look, then hurriedly squeezed back out through the bars and leaped to the ground. "Fangs a lot, big boy!" I snapped over my shoulder, then scampered off after her.

"Rita, wait!" I shouted, catching up. "I tell you, he talked! All about the woods, and getting caught, and—"

She stopped and gave me a chilly look. "You just can't hack being out of the limelight, can you, Gramps?" she sneered. "Talk about a pitiful cry for help."

I practically fell over! "Is that what you think this is about? Me trying to get attention?"

Rita shrugged. "What else? First you risk your bony old neck getting in the cage with that monster. Then you claim you can get him to talk! If you're not making it up to get attention, you're either dreaming—or nuts! Which is it?"

"Both—I mean, neither!" I stammered. Whoa, I really did sound nuts. "Please, Rita, you've got to believe me! The bear talked! I heard him with my own ears!"

"I think that pink hair dye's soaking into your brain. Now are you gonna step aside, or am I going to have to get ugly?"

"You mean uglier—and I don't think it's possible!" I growled.

A sudden sharp whistle from the door of the tent made us both look up. There was Mike, looking impatient. He spotted me, cupped his hands around his mouth, and hollered, "Pete! Here, boy! We're waiting for you!"

Horrors! The blasted cannonball! I caught Rita giving me a smug grin. Ooh, she was enjoying this much too much.

"Yeah, put some hustle on, Bone Breath!" she taunted. "Maybe a trip through the cannon will clear your head."

CHAPTER

11

The less said about the next few days, the better. If you were worried that they'd stuff me down the barrel with a bucket of gunpowder and light it for a send-off—no such luck. That kind of act has one big drawback. You can only do it once.

No, the contraption hidden in the barrel of the cannon is like a springboard with a trip wire attached. The smoke and boom are just for show.

Part of me had hoped that the clowns would accidentally launch me into the next county. That would solve my problems once and for all. But those boys knew their business. Two shows a day I was put into a cute little pilot's helmet and flight suit and sent zooming over the audience and into the net.

It didn't hurt and the crowds ate it up. So why did I hate it so much?

I'll tell you why. Pride! You might not think a dog has such a thing, but you'd be wrong. And mine was in tatters. All my talent and training? Totally wasted. A sack of cement could have done the cannonball as well as I did. Though it probably wouldn't have looked as cute in the helmet.

And it didn't help that Rita was the one who pulled the trip wire, grinning like a goblin the whole time.

Yep, I was trapped—trapped like a trap in a trap. Nothing short of a grade-A extra-large miracle was going to free me. I knew better than to hope for one.

And Fremont, you ask? Where was Fremont? Still holed up in his cage, pouting. I'd washed my paws of him since he'd made me look like a chump in front of the chimp. I took the long way around back to my trailer at night to avoid passing his cage. My route led through the back pasture where our humans were camped out.

That's how I happened to be outside the ring-master's trailer when he and Boston Charlie were talk-ing about Fremont after the evening show.

"He's gettin' worse instead of better, boss," Charlie was whining. "I can't make no headway with him at all. I think he's got a screw loose or something!"

"Then tighten it!" growled the ringmaster.

I paused outside the spill of light from the open door and cocked an ear. Was Charlie really throwing in the towel?

"But boss—" Charlie started, but the ringmaster wasn't having any.

"I paid good money for that monster, and I'm gonna make it back," he snapped. "You say he's got too much fight in him? Then cut off his food! I guarantee that'll gentle him—and fast."

Starve Fremont? I was so shocked that I sat down—plop!—right there on the grass. My jaw practically hit the ground along with my hind end.

Our trainers worked us with kindness, treats, and praise. They knew we'd always do our best for them because we wanted to please them. But starvation? That was not on the menu. At least not up until now.

I could hear a note of surprise in Charlie's voice when he replied, "The hunger treatment? I don't know, Rudy. I ain't never . . ."

"Yeah, and you ain't never trained a wild bear before, neither. The bill collectors are dogging me. Ticket sales are down. And that bear eats like a high school football team! I don't like the hunger treatment either, but I got no choice. No more chow—not one bite!—until he works, same as the rest of us."

I didn't wait for more, but sprinted off to find someone to tell.

The first animals I came to were the Lipizzaner mares. They were tethered and nibbling grass. Imelda shook her halter at me, annoyed.

"Peter, must you dash up on vun like zat? Is so rude, no?" Her sisters, mouths full, nodded in agreement.

But I had news and no time to waste. "They're gonna starve Fremont! The bear! I just heard the ringmaster say so!" I yipped.

If I was expecting her to show concern for a fellow four footer, I could have saved my breath. Imelda just went on grazing. I pranced right up under her nose.

"The hunger treatment, Imelda! Hello? Are you

getting this? Charlie's gonna use the hunger treatment!" I barked. She jerked her head away and stepped back.

"Honestly, Peter. Vhat vould ve care? It's not as zhough za bear is vun of us!" Sophie complained.

Her younger sister Czarina chimed in, "Za bear has asked for it, no? And now he vill get it. Unless you vhant ve should take him some grass?" All three of them threw their heads back and whinnied at that.

"Where are your motherly hearts?" I asked. "I thought you fillies were supposed to have a soft spot for kids in trouble!"

"If I had a foal as ugly as zhat one, darlink, I'd starve him myself!" Sophie cracked. This time they laughed so hard that Imelda swallowed her cud and had to blow through her nose to work it loose.

I don't mind telling you that I was shocked—shocked!—at this. Surely I'd find someone in the troupe who'd share my outrage at the ringmaster's cruel plan?

One thing became painfully clear as I made my rounds from coop to cage to kennel. Ol' Fremont wasn't going to get voted "most popular" any time soon.

In fact, as far as the rest of them were concerned, the ringmaster could have had him stuffed if the fancy took him. They wouldn't have lifted a paw, claw, or hoof to stop him. Even my fellow Performing Pups gave me the doggy version of a shrug.

"And anyway, Pete, what could we do, even if we wanted to do something?" Scrappy pointed out. The other mutts yapped their agreement. Then all of them stuck their noses back into their chow bowls and got on with dinner. Case closed.

But not me. "Maybe you bums can enjoy a meal while a fellow animal goes hungry, but I can't," I growled. "Bone appetite, boys and girls."

And with that I bent down to my own bowl, carefully gripped its rim in my jaws, and carried it out of the kennel. I heard Scrappy start out after me and Lolly call him back.

"Forget it, Scraps. Pete's been itching for a dog fight ever since I took over his act," she barked. If I'd needed another reason to leave, there it was. Bowl clenched firmly in teeth, I trotted off into the night. I was a dog with a mission.

I was gonna feed the bear.

CHAPTER 12

The meaty aroma wafting up from that bowl had me drooling so much, I was afraid I'd skid in it. But I made it to Fremont's cage. He was hunkered over in one corner, his back to me and the world.

"Herfe's fumfimg for youf," I managed to get out past the bowl. Carefully setting it down, I shoved it

through the bars of the cage. Some spilled, but most of the juicy nuggets stuck to the bottom. The bowl was a paw's reach from Fremont. But Fremont didn't even look around.

Self-sacrifice can be kind of fun when you get some thanks in return. I'd have settled for a grateful look. But Fremont, the big lump, was a bear of stone. He didn't budge.

"For heaven's sake, aren't you gonna eat it?" I growled.

"I'm not hungry," he said.

I snorted in disgust. "I sure wish I'd known that before I came all the way down here with my dinner bowl in my teeth!"

"Your dinner?" That got his attention.

"Whose did you think?" I sniffed.

He slowly turned around, reached a paw toward the bowl—then pulled it back again. "Aren't you hungry?" he asked.

"Nah," I lied, hoping my rumbling stomach wouldn't drown me out. "That cannonball act shoots my appetite."

Fremont swallowed that whopper easy enough and got my dinner down in the next gulp. One lick for the last tasty drops, and my bowl was as clean as a hound's tooth.

Fremont picked it up, turning it in his bulky paws with surprising ease.

"Why did you do it?" he asked, not looking at me.

"What? Share my dinner? I dunno," I admitted. "I don't think it's right to starve somebody to make him work. It's not the way things are supposed to be done around here."

"I'm sorry I embarrassed you in front of your friend," Fremont said, still goofing around with that bowl. "I just didn't feel like talking."

"No sweat," I assured him. "I don't care what Rita—"

That's as far as I got when Fremont did something I'd never seen anything outside of a chimp or a human do before—or since.

Sprawled on his back, he started flipping my bowl from one paw to another. My jaw snapped shut harder than a trap. Before I could say a word he began tossing it, whirling it into the air. Just like he'd been doing it all his life!

"Wha-, where—where'd you learn to do that?" I finally choked out.

"Do what?" Fremont yawned, glancing my way.

"That—that bit with the bowl!" I said. "You're juggling!"

"What, this?" Fremont snapped the bowl into the

air with a quick kick, sending it almost to the roof of the cage. He snagged it on one toe and gave it a spin with the other paw. He tossed it back and forth in big loopy arcs! He caught it on the tip of his nose and balanced it, before letting it fall to the floor with a clatter.

"It's just something I do, to cheer myself up," he

said with a shrug. "Catching one thing is cinchy. You should see what I can do with a bunch of pine cones."

Pine cones?!

"Wait right there!" I said—like he had a choice.

Squeezing out between the bars, I hotfooted it to our old wooden prop box. I nosed it open and dragged out three battered bowling pins. Next, I grabbed a big red and white striped rubber ball.

One by one I shoved the bowling pins through the bars to Fremont. He poked at them, snorting at their human scent. I was trying to work the rubber ball through the bars, when he picked up a pin and began flipping it from one paw to another.

Leaving the ball, I squeezed back into the cage, picked up a second pin in my teeth, and tossed it to him.

He caught it!

I grabbed up a third and threw it to him. Fremont fielded that pin like a pro. Then he sent all three of them sailing through the air: pop-pop-pop! And caught them! Around and around they went, as pretty as a Ferris wheel on opening night.

The kid was a natural. An honest-to-goodness born natural.

I couldn't help it. I threw back my head and yipped like a pup. Then I chased my tail a few laps for good measure. When I finally collapsed to the floor, panting, Fremont had frozen and was staring at me in amazement.

"Whoa, what's with you, Pete?" he asked.

I rolled on the floor, growling and snapping at the air. I bounced up and danced a little jig of joy on my hind legs.

"What's with me?" I was finally able to bark. "I'm Christopher Columbus—and I just fell over America! No! I'm that guy who walked on the moon! It's a whole new world! You!" I sprang into the air, straight at Fremont. He caught me as neat as a quarterback catching a winning pass. "You—you great big, bushy miracle!!"

Unable to contain myself, I gave him a big, wet doggy kiss right on the nose. Fremont dropped me like a hot rock. He stared at me like he thought I'd gone totally off my nut—which I had.

"Miracle?" Fremont repeated. "What do you mean?"

"You and me—that's what I mean! Pete and Fremont! The biggest thing to hit the big top since—since pink popcorn! Don't you see it, Fremont? You're it—

my second chance at first on the bill! A bear and a dog—it's never been done! We'll thrill 'em! No! We'll kill 'em!"

I saw the look on his face and added quickly, "I mean, in a nice way. Star quality, Fremont—that's what I'm talking about. If you're this good without training, imagine what you can be with a pro like me to coach you! I can see it now. Matching costumes, you on a bike—hey, can you ride a bike?"

Fremont, catching my excitement, nodded happily. "Sure I can! What's a bike?"

I waved a paw. "No matter. You'll pick it up in a jiff. If you can toss a bowling pin, you can toss me just as easy."

Fremont reached for me, eager to please. "You want me to toss you now?"

I jumped back. "No! I mean, when we start rehearsing for the show."

Suddenly the sparkle went out. "You don't mean a show for people, do you?"

I rolled my eyes. What did he think, for pigeons? "Well, yeah. The public. Our public!"

Fremont glared at me, then turned his back. He hit the floor with a boom that sent hay flying.

"Forget it. I already told you. I hate people. I don't want to be a show."

What?! This could not be happening. I wouldn't let it! Was my rosy future doomed to go up in smoke yet again?

"You gotta, Fremont! It's my only—I mean, your only chance to keep from getting the hunger treatment! To save the circus!"

"Don't care," growled the big heap of stinking fur.

I was starting to lose it. "They'll starve you! And don't count on me to bring you my breakfast, either!" I warned him.

"Don't care."

"They—they'll put you in a zoo, Fremont! Behind bars! Little kids will chuck peanuts at you! Cub Scouts!" It was brutal, but he had to hear the truth.

"Don't care," he grunted again, and added, "It can't be any worse than this place."

I lost it. "Fine! Starve! What do I care? The Lipizzaner fillies were right. You're an amateur! A hick from the sticks! I wash my paws of you!"

Fremont lurched to his feet, an angry glint in his eyes. "Good! How about I toss you back to your tent?!"

I beat it out through the bars just ahead of his big, helping paw.

I didn't even look back as I walked away. You can lead a bear to water, but you can't make him drink—much less ride a bike. Game over.

And I guess that's where we would have left it—me in the cannon and him in the cage—if it hadn't been for a summer storm, a pile of dry hay, and a tiny little spark.

CHAPTER 13

We were camped that week on a pasture that backed up to a field of hay stubble. It was hot. That stifling, steamy sort of hot that feels like being rolled in a wet wool blanket. The sweet, green grass of June had been baked into Shredded Wheat. Between shows, I crawled around looking for a sliver of shade to flop in and dream of dropped snow cones.

There wasn't a breath of breeze in the big top that day. The scattering of people in the bleachers barely had the energy to put their hands together. And we didn't give 'em much to clap for.

Our troupe stumbled through their paces like they were sleepwalking. It's hard to keep up the oomph when you're melting like wax under the spotlight. For once I was glad to skip the flaming hoop. At least being Canine Cannonball, you get a nice wind through your fur.

The evening show wasn't any better. Lucky fell asleep and toppled off his stool smack in the middle of the big-cat act. Some of the audience laughed. But Boston Charlie got so flustered he gave Lucky a little flick on the butt with his whip. Lucky actually leaped up and roared like he meant business.

Poor Charlie!

First Fremont chased him up a pole, now good old Lucky? Lucky felt bad right away and went through the rest of his paces as sweet as a kitten. But you could see that Charlie was wondering if it wasn't too late to get into another line of work.

Nobody had much of an appetite for chow or chatter afterward, so we all dragged off to our various beds, cranky and wrung out. The idea of listening to the other dogs grumble and shift around on their pillows all night didn't appeal to me. But I could hear distant thunder, and sleeping out in a storm sounded even worse. I settled into my basket, found a cool spot, and went out like a light.

The storm rolled in late, with lightning that made the air sizzle and snap. The way Fremont told it to me afterward, he woke up all of a sudden without knowing why. The thunder? It wasn't that. Bears are used to weather.

Something made his big head pop up, ears cocked and eyes searching the darkness for—what? He wasn't sure, not right then. Not for the seconds it took his sleepy brain to put a name to the smell biting at his nose . . .

Smoke!

Fremont got to his feet fast. Smoke means fire, and fire is something that even a grizzly fears. There it was—a red flicker in a pile of dry hay just beyond his cage. As he watched, it flared into flames. Startled, Fremont roared. Everything in him was screaming to run, run, run, or die.

He grabbed the cage door and shook it. The hinges creaked and rattled but didn't budge. The fire was spreading fast. It greedily licked the dry grass, swallowed a tree.

With strength even he didn't know he had, Fremont wrenched the cage door again. The wooden frame gave way, splintering into toothpicks. The iron-barred door fell with a thud. Fremont was free!

He bounded away. His instinct drew him toward a

river he could smell in the distance. All of us were asleep in our trailers and lean-tos. There was nobody to stop him.

But he didn't run.

Eyes stinging from the smoke, Fremont started back toward the animal trailers. His nose was working overtime to sniff out the scent that would lead him to . . . me.

When he found the dog trailer, Fremont didn't waste time knocking on the door. He just ripped it off its hinges like you'd pull the top off a candy box. That got us up!

When my fellow pups saw who our visitor was, they backed up to the wall pretty quick.

"Fire!" Fremont told me, coughing. That one word was all it took. I'd never been through a circus fire, but we've all heard of them. Short of a tornado, there's nothing worse.

No time to waste! I scooted past Fremont, barking over my shoulder at Lolly, Scrappy, Arthur, and the rest to hurry up and follow me.

Outside, we could see the glow over by the haystacks growing brighter as we watched. Scrappy whined, eyes wide.

"Not now," I snapped, though I was as scared as he was. "Got to get the others. The rest of you, go get the humans! Fremont, come with me!"

The Lipizzaner sisters were already awake, staked out closer to the fire than our trailers were. I could hear their shrill neighs and angry snorting. I ran as fast as my four legs could carry me, Fremont right behind.

The horses were jerking their heads around, trying to pull up the stakes that trapped them there. The fire had spread, and three dry haystacks were going up like—well, like dry haystacks. In the flickering light, the mares' eyes were wide and wild. When they saw Fremont, their whinnies turned into screams. I danced around their stumbling feet, trying not to get stepped on.

"Don't be scared," I yelled, hoping they'd hear me through their panic. "He's here to help! Fremont! Pull 'em loose!"

Ignoring the horses' nickering protests, Fremont grabbed the tie ropes in one ham-sized paw. He twitched the big stakes from the ground like he was pulling up daisies. Pop! Pop! Pop! Forgetting their manners, the horses beat it as quick as they could without so much as a thank you.

We were already on our way to the cages, anyway. I could hear Rita's shrill screech and Zamba's rumbling roar.

The big cats were pacing, tails twitching. Rita was clinging to the bars of the cage, her big, yellow teeth chattering. "Me first!" she screamed. "Me! Save me!" Fremont grabbed her cage door and popped it off.

I could hear an excited babble of voices down by the humans' trailers. The dogs had done their job. Somewhere in town, a fire truck siren squalled.

Fremont wasn't waiting around for help, though. Grunting, he was straining to wrestle the door off Lucky's cage. When it wouldn't budge, Fremont ran back and lunged at it, crashing into the bars like a runaway truck. Lucky crouched in the corner, not sure whether to be more afraid of the fire or his rescuer.

Voices behind us! Fremont turned, and there was Boston Charlie in a pair of silk pajamas. A big ring of iron keys was in one shaking hand. His gun was in the other. Others were running up behind him, slopping buckets of water. The ringmaster was yelling orders that nobody seemed to be listening to.

"Fremont," I yelped, "don't move!"

I saw Boston Charlie's gun hand coming up, and I jumped for it.

I got his pajama cuff in my teeth and held on. Charlie cursed and tried to pull free. The gun thudded on the ground, and I let go.

"Run for it, Fremont! Go!" I yelped, and got between Charlie and the gun.

But to my astonishment, Fremont just sighed and sat down. For a second, I thought somebody must have got him with another knockout dart. When he spoke, it was so soft I wasn't sure I'd even heard him right.

"Run where?" Fremont whispered. He let Boston Charlie and some of the others put irons on him. They led him away, and he followed as docile as if he'd been in chains all his life.

I watched him shuffle off, my heart in my mouth. They've finally done it, I thought to myself. They've broken the wild bear. He's come around. He's one of us. I should be happy.

So why wasn't my tail wagging?

CHAPTER 14

Thanks to Fremont and his wild-animal nose, nobody was hurt that night. I was grateful, and so were the rest of the animals. But were our humans?

In a word, no.

I hope I'm not stepping on anyone's paw here, but I have noticed that even your smarter than average human can be a little dense. Fremont was the hero who'd saved their circus, not to mention their hairless hides. Surely he should get a medal, or a parade, or even just an extra-large jar of honey?

What he got was a one-way trip to a new and improved cage.

It was at rehearsal the next day where we heard them talking about it. All of us were feeling kind of skittish, including the humans. The stink of smoke had soaked into the tent canvas. It would hang there for many long days to remind us of how close we'd come to losing our home. Even the Lipizzaner sisters, usually so cool, were on edge. Czarina missed a step during a dance routine and kicked her sister Imelda, who neighed angrily.

"Vatch it, you nag! You nearly tripped me!" she spat, nipping at Czarina's ear with a set of choppers the size of piano keys.

Czarina tossed her head. "Trip!? I give you trip— one-vhay trip to glue factory! And keep teeths to yourself, unless you maybe like bite of my hoof!?"

Well, I tell you, the talk between those girls was way beyond anything you'd want to see in print. Madame Suzette had a tough time holding them back.

She calmed Czarina, stroking her nose and whispering to her. But Imelda still fumed and stamped. Madame saw the ringmaster watching and gave a shrug.

"Vhat can you do?" she sighed, with a final pat to Czarina's neck. "Horses still nervous from fire, poor things. Thank heaven they don't hurt themselves pulling loose from stakes." I saw Czarina shoot a guilty look to Sophie and Imelda. They glanced away, suddenly quiet again.

The ringmaster nodded. "We're lucky Mike's pups woke up in time to alert us. Though how they got the door off that trailer, I'll never figure out."

I'd been resting, watching Arthur and Scrappy work on their tumbling routine. (People just love to see a little dog jump over a big one. Don't ask me why.) But this got me on my feet.

"We didn't, you big, dumb box of rocks!" I yipped—not because I thought he'd suddenly learned to speak Dog, but because I couldn't just sit there and listen.

"And it's a good thing that crazy bear didn't have enough sense to know he was loose," he continued. "Musta got knocked silly when that lightning bolt hit his cage."

Rita, working up on the slack rope with a parasol, let it fall. She neatly pegged the ringmaster right on the bean. He yelped, then glared up at her before stalking off, rubbing his head. Rita dropped on the sawdust next to me with an angry screech.

"That's it!" she snapped, eyes flashing like stoplights. "I don't know about the rest of you, but I can't

hang around and listen while the dogs hog all the credit!"

"Excuse me!? Dog—hog?!" I bristled. "We know it was Fremont who raised the alarm, but what are we supposed to do about it? Put an ad in the paper?!" The other pups barked in agreement.

Sophie Lipizzaner said softly, "It doesn't seem fair, za way zey talk about your bear. He is amateur, true, but brave." Her sisters nodded in unison.

"Sure, he's brave." I agreed. "Not to mention as talented a young fellow as I have seen in or out of the big top. Despite what some people say." I looked hard at Rita.

"Okay, fine, he's a diamond in the rough—the very rough," she snapped back. "But how were we supposed to know?"

PeeWee, who'd been sidestepping closer and closer, the better to butt in, suddenly piped up. "Hey, you guys! I know something!"

Rita curled her rubbery lip. "That is news!"

Offended, PeeWee fluffed out his feathers and turned to me. "Boston Charlie still can't get your bear to do anything, and the ringmaster says he's not worth feeding—"

"Boston Charlie?" Rita cut in, smiling sweetly. Pee-Wee stopped in midsquawk, goggling at her with those big golf ball eyes.

"No—the bear. And he said he's going to sell him—the bear, I mean—to the zoo, when we hit Missoula."

My heart sank. "That's in two weeks!"

Lucky gave a rumbling growl of sympathy that sounded like a boulder rolling down stairs. "Whaddaya gonna do? No play, no pay. That's show biz. Still, the zoo . . . your bear ain't gonna like that, Pete."

Rita nodded, then poked me in the chest. "Your bear's tied to the tracks, Bone Breath, and the train's coming. That's your cue to ride to the rescue."

"My bear? How did he get to be my bear?!" I demanded.

Rita raised her eyebrows in that creepy, almost human way she has. "When he decided you were the only one worth talking to. Course, he doesn't know you like we do."

"And how am I supposed to rescue him? Since I seem to have mislaid my super powers," I snorted.

"Not just you." Rita turned to the others. "The bear—Fremont?—saved us all. Now it's our turn to save the bear."

CHAPTER 15

Clearly Rita was cooking up a plan, but there was no time to dish it out now. We were packing up and moving on to the next town. The only thing you can count on in circus life is change.

Madame Suzette led the Lipizzaner sisters outside for their comb out. The clowns, who looked as plain as vanilla out of their greasepaint, worked alongside the acrobats to take down the big top. The ringmaster, shirt off, trotted around bawling orders and mopping his face with a red bandanna. Mike fed and watered us out by the truck that would carry us to the rail yard. Our circus train was waiting.

As we were eating, PeeWee came bucketing along. "Listen up, dogs!" he honked. "Rita says, meeting at midnight tonight on the train. Pass it on!" And he loped off to do so himself.

Greta picked up our empty food bowls, giving me a nice scratch on the head as she passed. The Lipizzaner sisters were clip-clopping up the ramp into their trailer. The big top was rolled up and being heaved-and-ho'd into the van. Most of the trucks and trailers were already pulling out on their way to the switching yard. Mike gave the whistle, and the Pups scrambled up the steps into the back of the camper, for the ride to the train. I was the last dog to load up and paused a moment to look back, like I always do.

Is there any place sadder than circus grounds after the circus has gone? We pack up our magic and move on. All that's left is a couple of torn ticket stubs blowing through the dusty weeds. Soon the grass will sprout up in the scars from the tent pegs. There won't be a trace left to show that we were ever there.

Greta got in and closed the camper door behind her. I heard the rumble of the engine starting, and we were gone.

Rita was as good as her word. That night she used her agile fingers to untie, unhitch, unlatch, or otherwise free every animal on the train. One by one, we walked, hopped, or flew into the baggage car. Pounding on a crate with an empty soda can, Rita called us to order.

"We all know why we're here. Fremont's in trouble, big trouble. He's on his way to the zoo." There was a squawk of horror from those who hadn't heard. She hushed them with a wave of her shaggy arm. "Why? Because he chose to save our show, when he could have just run off and left it to burn. A lot of us have held out on Fremont because he was an outsider. We've given him the cold shoulder, instead of a helping hand—or paw or hoof. Well, boys and girls, if he wasn't one of us when he came aboard, he is now. And it's up to us to see that he gets his break in show business."

"But he doesn't want to be in show business!" I protested.

Rita gave me a slow wink. "He will." She peered around, spotted a prop basket, and threw it open. Rooting around, she came up with three small rubber balls. She kicked the lid closed, then started off toward the end car, where Fremont was caged by himself.

I followed along with the rest of the troupe. I still didn't know exactly what Rita was up to, but it sounded like she had herself an idea—which put her one step ahead of me.

Fremont was curled up in his cage. The sound of all of us piling in got him up and rubbing his eyes.

"We're here to settle a bet, big boy," Rita said. Then she began tossing one of the rubber balls from hand to hand. "Pete says you can juggle. I say you can't."

I started to object, "But we never—oof!" A sharp dig from one of Rita's pointy elbows stopped me.

Before Fremont could answer, Rita cocked her arm and hurled that ball straight at his head!

Fremont didn't even duck. He just put up his paw and snagged the ball out of the air as smooth as a big league catcher. "Hey!" he yelped. "What are you—"

Fremont didn't have time to finish. Rita pitched the other two balls at him: Bang! Boom! Fremont fielded them just as neatly as the first.

"You better cut that out!" he growled, eyes narrowing.

Rita turned to me. "Okay, he can catch, but he can't juggle. No bear can juggle. Those big mitts are just too clumsy. Right, guys?"

The others had caught on to Rita's scheme, and they agreed.

"Nah, he can't juggle."

"Pete's off his nut."

Fremont snorted down his nose, scowling at Rita. "Gimme a break! Don't you think I know what you're trying to do? Like you're gonna get me to juggle, just to prove that I can?"

Rita wasn't giving up that easy. "Well—can you?"

"None of your business!"

"So, you can't? Or you can, but you won't? Or you can't, but you—"

"I can't—I mean, I can, but I can't, but I—you're giving me a headache!" Fremont clapped a paw to his head and groaned. I knew how he felt.

"Okay, all right!" He turned to me, holding out a ball. "But these are too easy. You know those things you gave me to play with before? The big ones?"

"Oh, yeah—bowling pins?"

He nodded. "Bring me some of those."

I heard a few impatient murmurs among the animals as I sprinted out to the prop basket. Rita tagged along behind me and together we hauled the pins back to Fremont's cage.

"This one time," Fremont growled at Rita. "I'll show you. Just to shut you up!"

And, bless his contrary little heart, he showed her. He showed them all, just like he'd shown me that day. He juggled with his front paws. He laid on his back and juggled with his hind paws. He juggled with all four paws, popping the pins off his nose. An enchanted chorus of *oohs* and *ahhs* arose from his four-legged audience. My heart swelled with pride.

When he finished, Rita led the applause as the rest of the animals stamped, yipped, and yowled their approval. Imelda was the first to speak up.

"Fremont, darling, you are mahvelous! Never have I zeen zuch a glorious talent! Pete, you sly dog, you should have told us!" she whinnied.

"But I did!" I squeaked.

Nobody paid any attention. They were too busy showering praise on Fremont, who had forgotten that he was too cool to care. He was melting like a caramel apple in the sun.

"Star quality—the kid's got what it takes! All he needs is a little coaching, some sequins, and a spotlight. He'll have 'em rolling in the aisles!" Zamba said.

Lucky nodded, yawning.

"Vhe can all help heem, no?" Czarina offered. "Cook up an act, show heem za ropes."

Rita pointed at me with a jerk of her thumb. "Pete here knows the kid best. I say they partner up, work out a routine together. Unless you're getting to like the cannon?"

I liked Rita's angle, but I had to wonder. Why this sudden interest in my career? It's not like we were pals.

Zamba frowned. "No offense, Pete, but is that the best idea? I mean, what with you having that little run-in with the hoop. Maybe you're not up to breaking in a new act."

I could see some of the rest of them agreed with him, though they didn't want to say it.

That got my hackles up. "Not up to it? That's a good one, coming from you. You get any fatter and you're gonna need a hoist to get up on your stool."

Zamba growled at that, and Rita stepped in. "Fremont's got the muscle, and Pete's got the experience. Pete needs a new act, and Fremont needs to learn the ropes. It's ideal! What do you say, Pete?"

Of course, I'd already thought of that myself. But it wasn't up to me. "I'm game, if Fremont is."

Fremont was lit up like a birthday cake, but now tried to cover it with a shrug. "Okay, I guess. If you really think I can do it—"

He was drowned out by a chorus of cheers.

Rita was already giving orders. "You'll have to rehearse nights, when the humans are asleep. Under the big top, in the ring. So Fremont can get used to it—"

I got it now. It wasn't about me. Rita saw a chance to boss us all around, and she'd grabbed it. Chimps love to run the show. Especially her.

"I don't want to rain on your parade, Rita, but have you taken a good look at the lock they've got on the kid's cage?" I asked. "Or did you plan to borrow the keys from Boston Charlie?"

Rita let out that earsplitting laugh of hers. She gave me a friendly sock on the shoulder that almost bowled me over. "As a matter of fact, Bone Breath, that's exactly what I had in mind. And guess who gets to help me?"

And so, Gentle Reader, began my life of crime.

CHAPTER 17

Okay, so it was more like a few evenings of crime. Not an actual life. But I was an honest, hardworking poodle who'd never so much as sneaked a nibble of another guy's kibble. Rita's plot made me feel as crooked as my own hind leg.

It wasn't until late afternoon the following day when we arrived at our next stop. Night was falling by the time the circus trucks were unloaded and the big top was set up. The humans were good and tired. Everyone hit the hay at ten o'clock.

I guess it was Rita's taste for drama that made her schedule our caper at midnight.

I tossed and turned in my basket, counting the distant "bongs" from the village clock tower. It seemed to take forever to get to twelve. But when it finally came, I wished it had taken longer.

Mike had tried to repair the dog trailer door. Lucky for me, he wasn't much of a handyman. The door opened easily when I pushed it with my nose.

I slipped out and crept silently through the shadows to Boston Charlie's beat-up, old camper. No sign of Rita yet. I settled in to wait for her, watching the sky as a woolly wisp of cloud gave the Man in the Moon a mustache. Rita's whisper made me jump. I barely stifled a startled yip.

The chimp was done up in a long, brass-colored wig. She wore a lavish coat of lipstick, some of it on her nose. I recognized her red ruffled dress as one of Lolly's costumes.

She looked like something out of a dream you'd have after eating bad Chinese food. I staggered back a step. Rita grinned. "Well? What do you think?"

"Why?" I managed to choke out.

She tossed her curls. "And you call yourself an artist? Where's your sense of style?"

I shook my head. "You've got enough for both of us."

"You got that right, Bone Breath. Let's get this party started." She pointed to a half-open window at the side of Boston Charlie's camper. "Put your paws on the sill and give a gal a boost."

I got up on my hind legs and propped my front feet below the window. My nose just reached the bottom glass.

"Can you see him?" Rita whispered impatiently.

"No, but I can hear him." I could have heard Boston Charlie snoring through a concrete wall. Rita ran up my back like it was a stepladder and perched on my shoulders. I opened my mouth to complain and nearly choked on a big, hairy foot.

In a flash, she had climbed over my head and was letting herself cautiously down into Charlie's bedroom!

I scrambled for a better view and managed to make out the hump under the covers that was our wild-animal trainer. Rita, moving like a career cat burglar, was already pawing through the stuff on Charlie's dresser. She slid open the drawers and searched through them with quick, quiet fingers.

"Try his pockets!" I hissed. Rita gave me a thumbs-up and reached for the trousers hanging on the bed-post. With one eye on Charlie, she jammed her hand in the front pockets, then the back.

Nothing!

She shook her head, making the curls dance.

"Look in his jacket," I whispered. "Over there, on the chair." Rita started for it, freezing in her tracks when Charlie let out a sudden, gulping snort!

Rita's eyes met mine and we waited. The seconds seemed to stretch before Charlie's chain-saw snore started up again. Rita blew a sigh of relief, then went for the jacket.

Left pocket—nothing. Right pocket—aha!

Rita held up the key ring to show me, then jammed it into her mouth. Quick as a wink, she was up and out the window and sliding down my back to the ground.

She spun the key ring around her finger. "Nerves of steel, that's me. If the circus ever gets boring, I could be a jewel thief."

Then someone sneezed in the next trailer, and we scampered away across the moon-silvered grass.

CHAPTER 18

I guess Fremont hadn't believed we'd find a way to spring him. The kid was bagging zs. My shaking didn't wake him. But when Rita shoved the key into the lock and the door swung open, he came to.

"Come on, Fremont," I said. "You're about to become a genuine overnight sensation!"

When we got to the big top, the Lipizzaner sisters were already waiting for us. So was Lolly. She'd pushed the big rolla-bolla ball all the way from the dog trailer, all by herself.

"I thought you guys might need this" she said.

I felt like a dirty dog after all the unkind thoughts I'd had about her. "Thanks, Lolly," I said. "You're a pal."

"Anything I can do to help?" she asked, ears up.

"Just stick around and give us pointers, okay? You are part pointer, aren't you?"

Lolly rolled her eyes. "Oooh! Down, boy. That joke's older than Lassie!" But her tail was wagging when she said it.

Fremont and I got to work—and work it was. All that attention he'd gotten last night had given the kid a swelled head. It was up to me to shrink it down to size.

The first hurdle was the rolla-bolla ball. Like a lot of things that look easy, walking on the rolla-bolla ball isn't.

I hopped on to give him a show how. "Keep it moving, kid! Slow down and you'll lose your balance."

Fremont yawned.

"Start out on four paws. You gotta work your way up to two!" I panted, neatly pivoting on the ball and coming back at him the other way.

Fremont stretched and gave me a smug grin.

"No biggie, Pete," he assured me, as I stopped and hopped down in front of him. "Bears have great balance."

To prove it, Fremont leaped up onto the ball just the way I had, and—whomp!—the ball skittered away.

I could hear snickers from the sidelines where the Lipizzaner sisters, Rita, and Lolly were watching. Fremont jumped to his feet and hunched his big shoulders, glaring at them.

"What are you laughing at?!" he snarled.

Sophie tossed her head impatiently. "You! You are very silly boy!" she scolded. "You zhink zat you do easy vhat it takes rest of us hard work to learn? Ha! In forest, maybe different. But here, Pete is master. You are only—only—?" She paused, looking for the right word.

"Dumb butt?" Rita offered helpfully.

Sophie snorted in disgust. "No. Pupil. Understand?"

Nobody can stare down Sophie Lipizzaner when she gets on her high horse, Fremont included. He dropped his head. "Yes, ma'am."

Sophie sighed. "Well, don't stand zere like cast-iron lawn stag, sveetheart. Get back on ball, try again."

Fremont turned to me. "Show me one more time, Pete. Please?" he muttered, sneaking a sidelong glance at Sophie. I smiled at him and hopped up for another spin.

"Sure thing, kid. Now, watch the paws. It's all in the paws."

The Lipizzaner sisters weren't there the next night—but Zamba and Lucky were. In fact, every night two or three of the troupe members showed up to help, offer ideas, and cheer Fremont on. Rita and I didn't miss a night, of course. How could we? No keys, no Fremont.

No Rita, no keys. Luck was on our side, though. Boston Charlie never budged an eyelid while Rita crept in to grab the keys or when she returned them just before dawn. (Thank goodness, she ditched her disguise after the second night.) Rita and I took turns grabbing catnaps during the training sessions.

The whole deal made me as nervy as a terrier, but Rita got a kick out of putting one over on the humans. Chimps aren't really happy unless they're making a monkey out of somebody.

After that first showdown, Fremont was as sweet as a teddy bear. I never saw an animal pick up tricks so fast. Not just the rolla-bolla ball, which he could sail around on after just a couple of nights. But the little comic bike, too, which Rita "borrowed" from the clowns. He mastered some flashy juggling tricks.

I made him practice with a bag of oats before I let him start tossing me around. Like I told you, I'm a full-sized dog, not one of your little, squeaky toy breeds. But in Fremont's big mitts, I looked like something you'd hang off your rearview mirror. In no time, I was leaping from paw to paw, jumping up on the handlebars of the bike, and riding on his shoulders while he juggled.

And Fremont? He was loving it. The action, the challenge, the fellowship with his new four-legged family. It was like he couldn't get enough. I practically had to drag him back to his cage when practice time was over.

Boston Charlie and the ringmaster couldn't figure out why Fremont wasn't buckling under with the hunger treatment. But they didn't see Rita making her nightly food collection rounds. There wasn't an animal in the show that didn't pitch in some of his or her chow. A bear will eat just about everything. And everything is what he ate, from Rita's bananas to Imelda's carrots. He even got a hunk of beef from Zamba, who nearly burst into tears as he shoved it through the bars.

A few afternoons I saw Boston Charlie lurking outside Fremont's cage. He was just looking him over, trying to figure it out. Once he caught me watching. I didn't care for the way his eyes narrowed as he studied me, like I was a piece of a puzzle he couldn't get to fit.

I went into my dumb-animal routine and pretended to be hunting a flea. Charlie tapped his coiled whip softly against his leg a couple times, chewed the end of his mustache, then stalked off.

Fremont grunted nervously. "There's something fishy about that guy, Pete."

"Yeah—his breath." I sniffed. "Sardine sandwich for lunch, I'd say."

"No, I mean it! I think he knows we're up to something."

"Boston Charlie? Please. That guy hasn't got a clue," I assured him.

But humans aren't always as dumb as they look.

CHAPTER 19

Truthfully, Charlie was the least of my worries. The biggest was costuming. Getting a costume in Fremont's size would have been like finding a party dress to fit Texas. We just had to improvise.

I rooted around in an old wardrobe trunk and came up with a blue, spangled bow tie and a matching pointy hat. Fremont was willing to go as far as the bow tie, although he growled that it choked him. But when he got a look at the hat, he shook his shaggy head.

"Nope. I'm not wearing that. No way."

"Yeah, way!" I snapped. "You're in show business, Fremont. You've got to show."

He folded his big arms and pouted, the big baby.

But when the others chimed in on my side, Fremont knuckled under.

Seeing the kid in costume, I was sure that the public was gonna eat us up. But first, we had to get ourselves on the menu. We had to make a splash, a big one, and that meant playing to a packed house. The last performance in that town would be on Saturday, always our biggest crowd of the week. Perfect! Fremont was ready. I was ready.

But there was one hitch. Someone would have to let us go on in their place. It was a dicey situation. If we wowed the audience, everything would be fine and the ringmaster wouldn't bat an eye. But if we flopped? There would definitely be trouble, for us and anyone who'd helped us out. Who'd chance it?

I was watching the clowns set up the cannon, when I heard Arthur clear his throat behind me. I turned to see him, Scrappy, and the rest of the act standing there.

"On behalf of the Performing Pups," Arthur began in his booming bark, "we'd like you to take our spot on the bill tomorrow night. So's you and the bear can do your stuff."

I choked up, I confess. These guys were willing to risk their tails for me.

"When our music comes up," he went on, "we'll run out like usual. Rita will sneak your bear out of the cage and put him on his bike. He'll ride in like it's part of the show, see? We'll beat it back to the wings, and you jump in and do your thing."

Lolly spoke up with a heartfelt "Pete, break a leg."

I know it sounds bad, but for a reason nobody can remember, it means "good luck" in the theater.

"Thanks, guys. I don't know what to say—I—'scuse me, but I gotta take a walk," I croaked, and scooted off so my pals wouldn't see me howl like a puppy.

Rita found me out behind the snack bar, comforting myself with a stray wad of cotton candy. She looked worried.

"Bone Breath, I've been thinking," she began. "Your bear is scared of people, right? Come tomorrow night, there's gonna be five hundred of them up in those bleachers. How can we be sure that Fremont won't choke up—or freak out?"

I just gaped at her. Cotton candy fluttered from my muzzle. I could hear the sucking sound of my dreams going down the drain. How could I have not thought of that?!

Oh, who was I kidding? I hadn't wanted to think of it.

Rita sighed. "Maybe we'd better ditch the plan—," she started. But suddenly the answer came to me in a blinding flash.

"Wait! The reason Fremont is scared of people is what?"

"Uh, because the ringmaster and Boston Charlie kidnapped him and threw him in a cage?" Rita guessed.

"Yes—I mean, no! The reason Fremont is scared of people is because he hasn't really gotten to know any nice ones, like Greta and Mike. If he could see humans like we do—"

"Friends, not enemies!"

"Exactly! Audiences, not attackers."

"Feeders, not food?"

"That, too." I put my head down on my paws, the better to steady my mighty brain. "If we could take Fremont to a place where he could see people, he'd see how cute and cuddly they are. You know, in their natural setting, playing with their young and stuff."

Rita shook her head. "Not if they see him first."

I gave her a big doggy smile. "I'm way ahead of you. Two words: night vision."

Rita rocked back on her bottom, lacing her toes together. "Okay, we can see well in the dark and humans can't. So you're saying—"

"I'm saying we take Fremont on the town—this town—late tonight. We stay to the side streets. We peek in some windows. Let him get an eyeful of their ways and a snoot full of their smells. Fremont gets used to them and—presto! No first-night nerves."

Rita was still shaking her head, but I could see she was leaning my way. "If this works, you're a lot smarter than I gave you credit for, Pete, ol' hound. But if it doesn't—"

"It'll work," I promised.

It had to.

CHAPTER 20

As usual, Rita lifted Boston Charlie's keys, and we slunk through the dark circus grounds to Fremont's cage. Lucky for us, it was a moonless, inky black night, perfect for the little caper we had planned. Fast as a flea, Rita unlocked the big iron door. Fremont was awake and on his feet, eager to go out and play.

"Change of plan, old bruin," I informed him. "School's out for tonight. We're going on a field trip to do some people watching. Kind of a sneak preview of your audience."

You'd think Fremont would have jumped at the chance for a night on the town with us, his two best buds. He jumped, all right—in the opposite direction.

"But I don't wanna!" he wailed, cringing in the far

corner of his cage. "Can't we just practice some more instead?"

"The act is fine, Fremont. It's you we're worried about. Stage fright can turn the best of us to stone, and the last thing I need is a petrified partner. Come on, have we ever steered you wrong?" I asked, ears up.

Fremont licked his nose nervously. "No," he admitted.

It was time for some tough love. "Then haul your hairy haunches out of that corner, you ungrateful cub, and march! That's an order."

And, to my surprise, he did.

The circus was camped out in a grassy pasture just east of the village. We could see its not-so-bright lights up ahead. I'd alerted the dogs to our plan, so there was no barking as we stole away.

Rita and I had agreed it would be best to stay off the roads. A car might come along, and no way was Fremont going to pass for a deer—or even a stray cow in need of a haircut. Cutting across the fields, we made our way to town.

But we were almost toast before we even got there.

An unfriendly farmer's dog saw us sneaking past his henhouse. He set up a racket that had the hens squawking and his master up and grabbing for his shotgun. I saw the farmer stumble onto his back porch in his underwear and caught the glint of the blue black barrel as he raised it to his eye.

"Drop!" I yelped, flattening myself in the grass. For once neither of them argued with me. A blast of buck-

shot zinged past us. We beat it out of there faster than
a pack of racing greyhounds, Rita wailing like a fire
truck.

Coming to the outskirts of the village, we came
upon a supermarket. An overflowing trash container
led me by the nose. Overripe baloney, rind of cheddar,
yesterday's chicken strips—it took all my willpower to
turn away. I nudged Fremont, who'd paused to inhale,

snout quivering. "No Dumpster diving tonight, pal. This is business."

Just as we'd hoped, the streets were deserted. The townspeople were snug in their various dens. We wandered at will down the quiet streets. Fremont's head swiveled as he took it all in. "What's that?"

"That's an apartment, Fremont. People live in them."

Fremont blinked. "They put themselves in boxes?"

"Well, yeah. They like 'em."

Fremont nodded thoughtfully. "That explains a lot."

Rita had gone on ahead. Down a pathway between two houses, we found her outside a lighted window, peering in. Fremont and I tiptoed over to join her.

It was someone's living room. A teenaged girl was sprawled on a sofa, talking on the phone. The television was playing cartoons, and two very sleepy-eyed little kids in pajamas were curled up in front of it.

"Those two should have been in bed hours ago," Rita said, frowning. Almost as if he'd heard her, the littler one looked up. His eyes focused on the window where we stood!

"Freeze!" Rita hissed. We froze.

The little boy got up and waddled to the window,

sucking on a soggy finger. As we stood there, trapped, he pressed his nose against the glass. He saw us, seeing him. His eyes went big.

"Ax! Dere a boh!" he gurgled excitedly, pointing at Fremont with a drool-soaked digit. "Boh!"

The teenager looked up. "What's he saying, Alex?" she asked the older kid. "What's 'boh'?"

Alex shrugged, never tearing his eyes from the set. "I think he said 'bear.'"

The teenaged girl sighed, rolling her eyes. "No more Goldilocks for you, Miles. Come on, you guys, bedtime."

She put down the phone, scooped up Miles under one arm, and grabbed Alex's hand with the other. This started a whole new discussion—a loud one—and we beat a retreat.

"See?" I said to Fremont when we hit the sidewalk. "Aren't they cute? And they just love bears."

"At least the little ones do," Fremont agreed.

This was progress! Rita and I traded a wink.

"They're all gonna love you!"

"Love me? Really?" Fremont marveled, clearly taken with the thought.

"Kid, if you were old enough, they'd run you for president," I assured him.

Fremont skipped ahead into a parking lot. A bright, blinking sign showed a red ball knocking down a big, white pin over and over. From inside we could hear a jukebox and the boom-boom-clatter of bowling.

Fremont put his nose in the air, sniffing. Hot

dogs and peanuts—I could smell them, too. Mmm, I thought, I'll bet they've got a Dumpster here . . .

While I let my attention wander, Fremont bounded up to the swinging glass door of the bowling alley. Rita brought me back to earth with a painful jerk to my tail. "Pete," she squalled, "he's going in!"

CHAPTER 24

This called for quick action! I flew at Fremont's backside, jaws open for business. Sssnap! I got a mouthful of bear behind and held on for dear life.

Fremont let go of the door—oh, joy!—and turned to swipe at me. It was all I could do to dodge his big paws while keeping my grip. Rita got there just in time to keep me from getting batted over the fence.

"Fremont, stop! There are people in there!" she screamed, leaping onto his shoulder and pulling his ear to get his attention.

Fremont stopped swatting at me to glare at her. "So? I could juggle for them! People love that, don't they?"

I let go of his rump. "Save it for the paying customers, kid." Clearly, our mission had been a success.

If anything, Fremont was too eager to get cozy with humans.

"Time to go home," I decided.

Fremont looked sulky, but he let Rita take his paw and lead him away. I pranced a little ahead—the better to ward off any unplanned human encounters. I could hear Fremont chattering excitedly to Rita about the wonders he'd seen through the door. "They had pins—lots of them! And this guy was trying to juggle a big, black ball. But he dropped it and knocked the pins over . . ."

I headed around a dark corner and into an alley. I was halfway down it when a pack of rangy, mean-eyed mutts suddenly appeared out of the shadows and blocked my way.

The leader looked like a cross between a bull-mastiff and a Shetland pony. He walked around me, sniffing rudely. "Hey, check this out, boys!" he growled. "Would you call this a dog?"

That got a laugh from his posse. One of them piped up, "That's no dog, Spike. It's a powder puff!" More snickers from the pack.

The boss dog, Spike, sneered, giving me a full view of his oversized choppers.

"Whaddaya say, Powder Puff? Wanna play?"

I smiled even wider, hearing my posse just turning the corner.

"Sure," I agreed sweetly, "but my buddy Fremont wants to play, too. Oh, Fremont?!" I called over my shoulder.

The thugs looked past me, probably expecting a Chihuahua. Fremont stepped into the spill of light from the street lamp. When he saw the dog pack, he rose up on his hind legs and roared loud enough to tremble the windows above.

You could see those curs were sorry they'd messed with me. But they didn't stick around to apologize. In fact, they practically trampled each other in their rush to escape. And Spike was leading the retreat.

I was dancing around Fremont's feet, yipping a song of triumph, when a window suddenly opened above us. An angry voice called out, "Quiet down there!"

Apparently Fremont didn't feel like being quiet. He threw back his head and bellowed even louder. Wincing, I looked up just in time to see a human head poke out of the window. The human's face registered shock and the human's voice screeched at the top of its lungs, "*Bear!*"

The neighbors rushed to their windows to see what the ruckus was about. They started yelling, too. Seconds later a siren was screaming up the street behind us.

"Boys!" Rita yelled over the hubbub. "I think it's time to make like the wind!"

We blew.

The three of us pelted down the alley and up

another one. That siren was getting closer by the second. At the far end of the street a big truck marked AN-IMAL CONTROL squealed to a halt, blocking our way. A fat guy in a brown uniform tumbled out of the passenger side. He was clutching a rifle. He stopped and stared at the three of us, flabbergasted. Clearly the bear, chimp, and pink poodle situation was not one they'd covered in his training class. The driver, a little guy, scrambled out after him, sputtering, "Shoot 'em, George! Go on and shoot 'em!"

Fremont rose upon his hind legs and roared at them. That was enough for George. He raised the rifle and pulled the trigger. Fremont suddenly moaned and tumbled over.

"Fremont!" I leaped onto his chest and breathed a mighty sigh of relief to see a tiny silver dart—not a bullet hole—lodged in his fur.

Rita plucked it out and sniffed it, making a face. "Tranquilizer. He'll have a grizzly-sized headache when he wakes up, but at least he will wake up."

Suddenly a net sailed through the air and dropped on top of us.

Our night on the town was over.

Like we say in show biz, there's no such thing as bad publicity.

Our field trip with Fremont turned out to be a public relations bull's-eye. Rita, Fremont, and me weren't just on the front page, we *were* the front page! *"Grizzly Panics Prattville!"* screamed the headlines. And there was a photo of Fremont out cold on the pavement. George, the Animal Control guy, was standing over him like the winner of a boxing match.

Rita and I weren't even mentioned until the second paragraph, "along with two other escapees from the Circus Martinez, a trained chimpanzee and a performing poodle."

But the box office was sold out by noon the next day. People were lined up begging for standing room. The ringmaster had said a few choice words about the fine he had to pay to spring Fremont and us out of jail. But now he wanted to let Fremont loose to terrorize the next town on our tour! Boston Charlie talked him out of it.

Fremont wasn't awake in time for the matinee. I went through my cannonball routine worrying about him and our act. Would he come to in time? Performing on the rolla-bolla ball called for a clear head and steady paws. So did tossing a poodle around, especially when that poodle was me. What if he had a headache? Or an upset tummy? What if he saw two poodles where there was just one? I took my bows along with the clowns, then dashed offstage to check on him.

But Fremont was still hibernating and didn't budge when I barked. I went to my trailer and let Greta take off my little spangled jacket, then hopped up onto the grooming stool. I tried not to whine as she combed through some nasty foxtails, tokens of last night's adventure.

After the matinee crowd had finally hit the exits, we all headed back to our trailers to rest for the evening performance. Lunch was served—my favorite, chopped chicken livers à la Mike. I hit the ol' feed bowl with a vengeance. There's nothing like a near-death experience to give a guy an appetite. And I'd had several in the last few hours.

"Big night, eh, Pete?" Scrappy asked.

I nodded, swallowing. "Not much of a town, but we gave 'em something to remember us by."

"What's it like, being out? Running free?" Arthur wondered wistfully.

I paused to think it over and eat another mouthful. "Either fun in a scary way or scary in a fun way. Until they drop the net on you, anyhow."

"Tell us about the dog pack again!" Bob begged. I was getting set to launch into my showdown with Spike one more time, when Rita bounced in. Her brow was creased.

"Houston, we have a problem," she began. "It's your bear."

Fremont?! "What? Did he wake up?" I asked.

Rita gave me a grim nod. "Yep. And if he means what he says, he may hold the record for the shortest career in show business."

Fremont was pacing his cage, grumbling to himself, occasionally letting rip with a roar that made the circus grounds ring. As I ran up, he stopped pacing to look at me. If his eyes could have shot lightning bolts, I'd have been one grilled hot dog.

"Fremont—" I began, then ducked. He swatted his water bowl against the bars and drenched me. "Hey!" I yelped. "What was that for?!"

"Get away!" he thundered back. "I hate you! And you, too!" Rita had just come up behind me. "Look, I understand you're a little miffed about getting shot and stuff," I replied as sweetly as I could. "But believe me, after they see our act tonight—"

"There's not going to be any act!" Fremont said, cutting me off. "I don't care if they send me to the zoo! I never wanted to be in your dumb act, anyhow. The stupid old circus stinks, and people stink, and you stink, too!"

"But, Fremont!" I could see my future going from bright to bleak. "You don't know what you're saying! After all our hard work—!" I swallowed hard. I didn't want to beg, but I couldn't stop myself. "It's not just you, Fremont. It's me, too! We're a team!"

"Not anymore! Now get away from me. And stay away!"

CHAPTER 23

Discussion over. I walked away with Rita beside me. Fremont's roar was still ringing in my ears.

My head was swimming. All my work, my hopes, the success that had been a whisker's breadth away? Gone, finished, history. At that moment, being eaten by a bear didn't sound so bad. It might even be an improvement. I wondered if Fremont would consider putting me on the menu.

Rita reached over and scratched me gently behind the ear. "Maybe he'll come around," she said. I shook my head.

"All signs point to no, as the Magic 8 Ball says." I was trying hard to sound breezy. But my heart was a chunk of clay in my chest. "Hey, things happen. Life goes on. Maybe it just wasn't meant to be." I was starting to run out of clichés. Why didn't she go peel a banana or something?

"But what will you do?" she asked, in a kindly way that somehow made me feel worse instead of better.

"Do? Canine Cannonball, of course. Until they send me to a nice, soft basket at the Old Animals' Home. I'll sort my clippings, chew over old times with the other fossils—maybe take up chasing golf balls."

Rita's sharp little eyes searched my face. "And give up show biz? You? After all the work you've put into your act with Fremont—"

"There is no act, Rita." I could feel a tremble coming into my voice. I swallowed it down. "And what's the big deal about show biz, anyway? Just think—no more itchy costumes. Lots of nice, long naps . . ."

"Yeah, that would be sweet." Rita tried to sound like she meant it.

"Speaking of naps, I think I'll catch one right now," I said. "You know how it is when you get to be my age."

Rita opened her mouth to say something, then thought better of it.

I gave her a little nod and strolled off to find some quiet. A patch of soft, freshly turned earth under an old apple tree looked just right. I walked around it three times, flopped down, and shut my eyes. All I wanted was sleep.

I slept.

The sun was going down when I woke up. Uh-oh—how long had I been asleep? My head was buzzing and my mouth was as dry as a wad of wool. When I got up, my joints cracked like popcorn. Blinking the sleep sand out of my eyes, I trotted off toward the trailer.

Everyone was already inside, getting suited up for the act. Greta saw me and snapped her fingers, irritated. I hopped up on the grooming stool—it took two tries—and she got busy fluffing my pom-pom.

Scrappy was on the other stool getting his trademark big black eye painted on. "We heard about Fremont, dawg," he said, out of the corner of his mouth. "That bear's a looney tune. You're better off."

"Scraps, hold still!" Mike complained.

"Born an amateur, always an amateur," Arthur chimed in.

"Maybe you could come up with another act—" Lolly began.

"Thanks, but no thanks," I snapped, more sharply

than I meant to. "Zamba was right, I'm not up to it. You know what they say about old dogs and new tricks. Now, if you'll excuse me, I need to get into character for the Cannonball." I stared coldly into the mirror.

I could feel the others trading *what's with him?* looks behind my back. But nobody was eager to get his nose bitten off, so they kept quiet.

That suited me fine. I was the Canine Cannonball. And the Cannonball works alone.

When Mike whistled, we all trotted out of the trailer and around to the performers' entrance at the back of the tent. The band was playing "La Paloma," so I knew the performing pigeon act was wrapping up. Applause, applause. Then the band launched into a cheesy version of "The 1812 Overture"—dah-doo, dah-diddle, dah-dah doo-doo-boom. I could hear the clowns rolling in my cannon. The audience was laughing and clapping along with the music.

The music stopped and the ringmaster's voice rang out, "The most amazing feat of doggy derring-do ever presented, ladies and gentlemen, children of all ages, the Circus Martinez presents—the Canine Cannonball!"

The band struck up my theme song. Mike held open the tent flap. I could see the colored lights tumbling

over the sawdust, the clowns
rollicking, and the eager crowd
in the bleachers. I took a deep breath through my nose.
I could smell the sweet, familiar blend of sawdust, popcorn, and stands packed full of people. Mike gave me
my cue—two sharp, soft whistles. And I dashed out

into the ring, leaping into the arms of the biggest clown as the audience applauded.

Baldhead Billy was stuffing me into the mouth of the cannon when the audience began to shout. Startled, Billy turned to see what they were hollering about. And to my astonishment, he left me in the cannon and ran!

He wasn't the only one.

Every clown in the troupe was right behind him.

Alarmed, I struggled to free myself. What in the world had spooked the clowns? I tumbled from the barrel into the sawdust, then leaped to my feet.

I looked behind me—and practically fell over!

CHAPTER 24

It **was Fremont!** Fremont!

He was all gussied up in his glittery hat and swinging around the ring on the rolla-bolla ball like he'd been born to do it! I shook the sawdust off me and leaped toward him. My heart was singing!

The crowd was going berserk—stamping, shouting, thundering their approval. I jumped into Fremont's arms and onto his shoulders. Together we circled the ring as the spotlight danced over us.

The ringmaster turned three shades whiter, sprinted into the lion cage, and slammed the door behind him. The band didn't have a clue what to do. They swung into "Hold that Tiger," which was probably as good a choice as any.

As we whirled by the wings, I could see the rest of the animals huddled together and cheering us on. Our humans were standing there with their eyes popping out of their heads.

"I thought you were headed for the zoo!" I spluttered.

Fremont rolled his eyes. "What, and not be a show biz?"

And how were we, you ask? How was the Pete and Fremont Show?

We were—and this ain't carny barking, buddy—magnificent, colossal, and stupendous all rolled into one perfect package. We were the greatest thing since pink popcorn! Rita wheeled out the little comic bike and Fremont hopped on. He started flipping those bowling pins in the air as he pedaled. The audience was on its feet, hollering itself hoarse. Nobody had ever seen anything like us, before or since.

When we finished up and took our bows, the cries for "Encore!" were enough to flutter the canvas roof. The Lipizzaner sisters were waiting in the wings and had to ride out into our applause.

"Remind me never to follow you two again!" Sophie said as she trotted past, but she was smiling.

When we got to the wings, the rest of the troupe

was all over us—hugging, kissing, congratulating. Fremont just stood there, grinning like a goof and lapping up the praise like honey. My tail was fanning so hard I nearly made liftoff.

Fremont and I weren't the only ones being praised. I heard some human voices behind me, and turned to see the ringmaster, Mike, and Boston Charlie. From what I could tell, Mike and the ringmaster thought that Charlie had cooked up this whole thing as a surprise. Mike was busy congratulating him. Charlie was just standing there, dazed. His mouth was moving a little but nothing was coming out.

The ringmaster was clapping them both on the backs hard enough to knock the air out of them.

"Just listen to 'em!" he kept saying, his big round face shining like a clean plate. "I don't know how you did it or when—but you did it!" Then he glanced over to where us animals were standing and frowned. "But, Charlie, shouldn't you put that bear back in his cage? Just in case he gets to feeling mean again?"

Charlie looked over at Fremont, and his face dropped like a stone. Reaching for his whip he edged toward us. Fremont caught sight of him, and I could see the fur on the back of his thick neck rise.

"Fremont," I whispered. "Go with Charlie. Let him put you to bed. From now on, we're all one big, happy family. Right?"

Fremont gave me a dirty look, but dropped to all fours and slowly started for his cage. Charlie walked along beside him, like a man in a dream. I followed and watched as Fremont stepped into his cage and let Charlie lock him up. Charlie stared at him for a long moment, his face working. He looked at the keys in his hand as if he thought they'd been playing tricks on him. Then he slid the key ring into his shirt pocket and buttoned it down tight. From the look in his eye, I knew that our days of snagging those keys any time we wanted to were over. Then he went slowly weaving off toward his trailer, mumbling to himself.

We were due to move on that night after the show. It wasn't until the wee hours that we were loaded on the train and on our way. Rita decided that Fremont and I deserved a party. As soon as the humans had gone to bed, she got busy letting everyone out of their cages.

In no time the baggage car was packed with animals jabbering at each other excitedly. Everyone wanted to tell his version of the amazing moment when Fremont had rolled out to stop the show. Imelda Lipizzaner rapped a hoof on the floor for quiet. The gang settled down.

"I sink I speak for everyone, Fremont, vhen I say zat tonight a star is born! When you came, you vere nobody. Tonight, you are vun of us. Vhelcome to our family, our tradition, our heritage. Vhelcome to—circus!"

Such a cheer rose up. Such a whooping, barking, and roaring of support. I could feel myself misting up.

"Speech, speech!" Zamba rumbled, and the rest picked up the cry. Fremont looked around.

"I never had so many friends before." He turned to me. "When I first got here, Pete was so nice to me. He did everything he could to help. And I just wanted to do something back." Suddenly shy, he shrugged, bobbing his head. "You talk, Pete. I—I don't know what to say."

Well, I didn't either. But I said it, anyhow. I talked about circus, and second chances, and dreams that really do come true.

Rita was leading the gang in song when I finally took a breath and looked around. Where was my partner? I put my nose to the floor and followed it, out of the baggage car and into the corridor. Everyone

was so busy bellowing out
the refrain, they didn't see
me go.

There, in the darkness, I
spotted him. He was standing with his nose pressed
against a high, narrow
window. Hearing my
footsteps, Fremont
turned to me. There
was something in
his eyes that made
my chest suddenly
feel tight.

"What is it, Fremont?" I managed to get out.
"What's wrong?"

Without speaking, he bent and gently lifted me up,
until my muzzle was at the window alongside of his.
"Sniff," he whispered.

I sniffed. Pine trees, damp earth, the tang of icy
spring water. I squinted into the distance. Dark,
rounded shapes rose against the far horizon.

"My mountains," Fremont said simply. A tear slid

from one glistening eye, glinted on cocoa-colored fur. "My home."

Home.

Such a little word, yet it hit me like a hurled brick. You can only dodge the truth for so long. Sooner or later, it comes back to bite you. Fremont didn't want to be a star. He didn't want to be circus. He just wanted to be—home.

Why hadn't I seen how miserable he was? I knew the answer to that one. Again, I hadn't wanted to see. Partnering with Fremont was my chance at getting back on top, to show the world I was still a star. I'd fooled myself into thinking he was happy, because I needed him to be. But Fremont needed something else. Something the circus couldn't give him.

I looked up at Fremont, his black nose making a steamy circle on the glass. He stared at his mountains the way a starving thing stares at food. He was starved, I realized, starved to the soul. And what had I offered him? A sparkly hat and a crummy bowl of kibble.

I had told him I'd be his friend.

Well, it was time to get started.

I slid from his paws and jumped to the floor. He

didn't notice, didn't even look around. Squaring my shoulders, I trotted back to the baggage car.

Now that Charlie knew we'd been snagging his keys, simply letting Fremont loose one dark night was not an option.

A lot of dogs might have given it up as a lost cause.

But Pierre Le Chien is made of tougher stuff.

Already, my keen doggy brain was chewing over a plan.

A plan to free my partner and send him back to his mountain lair. And not just your average, ho-hum great escape. Something larger than life, like Fremont himself. Something with . . . pizzazz.

I could see it now.

A daredevil act, a showstopping scheme that would make a new kind of circus history.

That is, if we could pull it off. It would take heroic sacrifice from every animal in the show. Split-second timing and nerves of steel. Not to mention more luck than it takes to win the lottery. And I'm the one who'd have to talk them into risking everything.

Piece of cake.

CHAPTER 25

When I laid out Operation Wild Thing for the others, I was expecting to hear some doubts. But not a flat-out no.

"I'm already an endangered species!" Zamba protested. "Why press my luck?"

"Yeah!" Lucky agreed, suddenly wide awake. "What if Charlie's got real bullets in that pistol he's packing? A cat could get hurt!"

"Out of zah question!" whinnied Imelda. "Our professional reputations vould be ruined!"

Even PeeWee was shaking his beaky bean. "I was hatched in Oklahoma!" he honked. "I don't know what wild is. I can't even spell it!"

I'd hoped for support from the Performing Pups,

but I didn't get it there, either. "Mad dogs, that's
what they'll call us,"
Arthur growled
darkly. "And
we all know
what they do to
mad dogs, don't
we?" A grumble
of agreement rose
up from the rest.

Rita had lis-
tened quietly to
all the protests.
Her beady little
eyes darted from one of us to the other. Finally she
spoke. "They're right, Pete. We're just circus performers. All we're good for is jumping through hoops or
walking on our hind legs. We couldn't pull it off if we
wanted to."

The nods and grunts of agreement from the rest of
them suddenly dried up like the Sahara. Czarina gave
an outraged snort and tossed her head.

"You are speaking for yourself, I sink?" she demanded, blazing down at Rita.

Rita blazed right back. "Don't get your tail in a twist, sister. I'm just telling it like it is. What Pete needs are animals that can play parts and make the audience believe them. Actors, not acrobats. You gotta have training, technique . . ."

"Perhaps you did not know my sisters and I toured one season with road company of *Aïda,* pulling chariot," snapped Sophie. "Zis is acting, no?"

"No," Rita agreed, innocently beaming back at her. "That's four-footed scenery." There was more muttering among the animals and some sideways looks at me.

Zamba lifted his paw and studied it. "Of course, if we wanted to," he purred, "we could give them a sample of our . . . savage sides." He suddenly sproinged out his claws and everyone jumped. He smirked, tickled by their reaction. "See? That's acting. Getting in touch with your inner cub."

I could have licked Rita's ugly, wonderful face then and there. "Acting? Ha! We're pros! You're right, Zamba. Hey, look at me, I'm shakin' already! One night, that's all I'm asking. One night, to give Fremont a chance to get home. And we'll give the greatest performances of our entire careers!"

That got them going! (A word of advice here, Gentle Reader. If you ever want a performer to go your way, just grab him by his vanity and the rest of him will follow.)

Rita peered at them, blandly shaking her head, then turned to me. "All right, Bone Breath, looks like I'm outvoted. You got yourself some actors." Then she gave me a long, slow wink.

When Rita and I told Fremont what was going to come down, he couldn't believe it.

"They'd do that, for me?" he gasped.

"Circus folks take care of their own. And once you're in, you're in," Rita explained. "Even if you're out. And come tomorrow night, you're out. If you're sure that's the way you want it."

Fremont turned to me, worried. "But, Pete—what about you? What will you do?"

"I've been thinking about that, too," I admitted. "About the whole second chance thing. How I needed to prove to everyone that I was still a star. And we showed them—boy, did we!" I grinned, remembering the roar of the crowd. "I just don't think it gets any better than last night. And that's good enough for me."

Fremont reached out a burly paw to pat my head. "We'll still be friends, though, right, Pete?" he asked softly. "Even if I'm not a—a show biz?"

"The very best," I agreed. "Now, let me tell you about our new and improved act."

*   *   ★   *   *

My plan was simple. There were no set parts to play. Everyone would make them up as they went along. The only thing they had to do was to wait for my signal, then let go.

There was a weird, unreal kind of feeling at rehearsal the next day. Rita kept bursting into nervous shrieks, setting my teeth on edge. All of us animals were as jumpy as kangaroos. Even the humans could sense it.

"Aren't you gonna work the bear today, Charlie?" I heard the ringmaster ask.

Charlie looked skittish. "Nah, I don't want to overwork him, boss," he said. "Him and the dog, well, they seem to have it figured out pretty good on their own."

The ringmaster chuckled. "Whatever you say, Charlie. You're the wild-animal expert." He strolled off, and Charlie shot me a fishy look. I just sat there, my tongue lolling out of my mouth, tail thumping the sawdust.

Charlie checked around quickly to make sure nobody was watching, then leaned toward me. "I don't know who it was that trained you and that bear, mutt," he hissed, "but I'm gonna find out. No dog is gonna make a monkey outta Boston Charlie!"

I just batted my big baby browns. I guess it must have hit him how odd he looked talking to me, because he suddenly pretended like he'd bent down to tie his shoe. Then he straightened up and strode away.

Rita bounced off the trampoline and landed in a heap next to me. "I'm starting to worry about ol' Charlie," she giggled. "I think he's a couple bananas short of a bunch."

I allowed myself a little smile. "When we finish with him, he'll be the whole fruit salad."

CHAPTER 26

Somebody from the local papers had gotten
hold of our reviews from the last town. (I might
be able to get my paws on the clippings, if you're in-
terested.) They ran the notices on page 1, with a nice
picture.

Ticket sales had soared, and now we were packed
to the rafters. Everyone wanted to see the wonderful
new bear and poodle act. They weren't going to see it,
of course. But I was pretty sure they wouldn't be
disappointed.

The ringmaster had made some last-minute
switches. Fremont and I now had the starring spot at
the end of the second half. That's where you put your
most important act, the one the crowd really came to

see. It was the icing on the cake, the realization of all my high-flying hopes. But it made me a little sad to think that we'd already taken our final bows. Who can say how far Pete and Fremont might have gone? Half-time at the Mega Bowl? Saturday morning TV? The world would never know.

We were twenty minutes into the first half of the show. I stood in the wings like a general, watching my troops move into position.

In the ring, Boston Charlie was working Zamba and Lucky, hardly bothering to crack his whip. Above them, Rita was stationed among the ropes and trapezes, along with Senora Paloma's pigeons. Czarina, Imelda, and Sophie were supposed to go on next. They were harnessed and in full costume a few feet from me. Pros that they were, the only sign of nerves I could see was the way Sophie kept flaring her nostrils and blowing.

They were all waiting for the signal.

PeeWee darted up to me and jammed his pop-eyed face down to mine. "I'm scared, Pete!" he squeaked, feather-duster eyelashes fluttering. "I can't do it! I just don't have it in me!"

I struggled for a way to get him going—short of

applying my teeth to his tail feathers. "Wild is a state of mind, PeeWee. Think of what Fremont would do, then just . . . be the bear."

PeeWee cocked his head. I could practically see the wheels turning in his bitty brain. "Be the bear . . . yeah. Got it. Thanks, Pete!" He trotted off with his eyes squeezed shut and muttering, "Be the bear, be the bear, be the bear . . ." I hoped he wouldn't hurt himself trying to climb a tree.

I checked over my shoulder. The Performing Pups were huddled together, quiet, watchful, and waiting. Everyone was in place. Everything was ready.

Time to party.

Taking a deep breath, I threw back my head—and howled!

Rita heard my signal. She thrust two furry fingers in her mouth and blew a whistle loud enough to stop every taxi within five miles.

In the cat cage, Zamba suddenly leaped off his prop stool and came down in front of Boston Charlie. He roared so close to poor Charlie's face that his hairpiece fluttered. Charlie fumbled and dropped his pistol, then dived for the cage door. His keys dangled from the lock.

Rita came swooping down and unlatched it for him, but kept the keys. Charlie tumbled out with Zamba and Lucky hot on his heels. Lucky leaped on Charlie, pinning him on his back. He bellowed in triumph as Charlie squirmed and squealed.

The Lipizzaner girls charged into the ring, harnesses flying. They began galloping in mad, sweeping circles. Madame Suzette chased helplessly behind them, shrieking in German. Overhead, Senora Paloma's

doves took off like little feathered fighter pilots. They let fly at the audience with their own special kind of bombs—Splat! Splat! Splat!

On my cue, the Performing Pups ran past me into the ring and up the bleachers. Barking at the audience, they added to the general racket.

Greta and Mike were trying with zero success to round up the Pups. Lucky still had Charlie pinned and was drooling all over his face. Charlie was hollering, "Help! He's drownin' me!" but nobody could hear him over the Pups' deafening barks.

And to top it off, here came PeeWee, working his wild side like nobody's business. Galumphing across the ring, he flapped his fanlike wings. He honked and snapped his big beak at the customers like he meant to eat 'em for lunch.

The ringmaster stood alone in the middle of it all. He turned slowly around and around like a man in a dream—or a nightmare—as the ticket holders ran for the exits.

Chaos, clamor, and confusion! Operation Wild Thing: Phase 1 was in full swing.

Rita, who had hopped onto Sophie's back as she

circled the ring, leaped off and landed at my side. "Lovely party, isn't it?" she smirked, fluttering her lashes and jingling Charlie's big key ring.

It sure was tough to tear myself away. But if Phase 2 was going to be a success, I couldn't hang around. I had bigger fish to fry—and a big bear to free.

Rita and I managed to shove our way through the crowds and out to the calm of our camp. Fremont was waiting in his cage.

"Wow, what a racket! How was it?" he asked eagerly.

"Everything we hoped, and then some." Rita unlocked the door, and Fremont stepped from his cage.

We picked our way past the beat-up trailers that housed our humans, slipping from shadow to shadow. Up ahead, we could see open fields. The three of us paused a moment to take in the view of freedom. The uproar of Operation Wild Thing raged on behind us. To me, it sounded like music.

Just then, I heard another sound. A cold, metallic click.

"All right, Pete—not another step, or I'll shoot you where you stand!"

Very slowly, I turned my head. There stood Boston Charlie. He was pasty faced, shaking with rage, and slimed with lion drool. He'd lost his hairpiece but he'd found his pistol.

And it was pointed straight at me.

CHAPTER 27

Fremont uttered a low growl, and Charlie turned the gun on him. "Tell your friend he better not try anything, dog, or else . . ."

"Stay still, Fremont," I whispered. "That thing Charlie's holding is no dart gun. Don't give him a reason to use it." I took a quick glance around. "Where's Rita?" Somehow the chimp had pulled a disappearing act.

"Shut up, dog! Oh, I know you're talking to that bear. I don't understand it—but you understand me, all right. Don't you, Pete?" Charlie moved closer to me, and I edged away from Fremont. "You understand everything—all of you! That's how you cooked up that new act of yours, isn't it? How you made a fool out of me! And this!" He waved at the tent with his free hand. "You cooked that up, too, didn't you?"

Charlie poked the pistol in my face, forcing me back a step at a time. "Yeah, you're a lot smarter than Mike and them give you credit for. But I'm on to you, pal. And it's payback time. Into the cage—now!"

"What do we do?" Fremont whispered, glancing over his shoulder. Behind us was a cage, its door open, just like it was waiting for us to show up.

"What he says." My heart was breaking. We'd come so close! But right now, the object was to stay alive. Together, the two of us slowly backed into the cage. Charlie jumped for the door, slammed it shut, and latched it.

Charlie sneered at us, raising the gun again. I swallowed hard, watching the little black eye of the barrel stare in my direction. "So much for your jailbreak. No dumb mutt is gonna make a jerk out of Boston Char—"

There was a whip crack of gunfire. I swayed on my feet, my eyes squeezed tight, and a roar filled my ears like an ocean wave. So this was what getting shot was like!

But why wasn't I falling over?

I opened my eyes and looked down at myself. No holes! Fremont was still standing, too. Boston Charlie had a baffled look on his face. Then his eyes went crossed and he hit the ground like a sack of sand. I could see a stainless steel dart stuck in his rear end. Rita stood a few yards away—with the ringmaster's tranquilizer rifle in her hairy hands.

She gave me a jaunty grin, casually tossing the gun over her shoulder. Unlatching the cage, she glanced down at Charlie. "At least we don't have to worry about waking him up."

The town we'd been playing was in the foothills. The scattered houses were easy to avoid, and we got busy putting distance between us and the circus grounds.

Soon, there were no houses in sight. As we went up into the hills, the human scent faded and I could smell pine trees and damp earth. We came to a dirt road and followed it. The mountains loomed ahead.

I don't know how far we'd gone by then, but my

paws were getting sorer with every step. And I was panting like a locomotive. As the sun sank, the shadows of the tall trees stretched longer and longer.

"Fremont, how much farther?" I asked, trotting to keep up.

"I'm not sure," he admitted.

We kept going. Now it was getting dark. The trees were bigger and closer together. And the dirt road was getting narrower by the minute.

Rita, who'd hitched a ride on Fremont's broad back, suddenly chittered with excitement. She pointed at a big, wooden sign a few yards ahead in the gloom.

"Unless I'm reading that wrong, I think we may be home free!" she chirped.

I squinted, trying to make out the words carved into the signboard. Then I grinned in relief and did a little hind-leg ballet, in spite of my aching dogs. "National Park! Fremont, you're safe! They can't come after you here."

"All the same, don't hang around in the open too long," Rita added. "You'd best get up into the backcountry. And we'd better head home."

Fremont sniffed deeply, closing his eyes. A big,

goofy smile spread slowly across his face. "Home," he breathed. He opened his eyes and looked at me. "You don't have to go back, you know. You could come with me. I could take care of you."

I smiled, but shook my head. "Home is where the heart is, my friend. And mine's back in that big, striped tent. I'd fit in around here about as well as a goldfish in a punch bowl."

"And last about as long, too," Rita said, scanning the underbrush uneasily. "Did you guys hear that—that crunching sound?"

"I'll miss you, Pete. I never had a friend like you before," Fremont said. He reached down a big paw. I put mine in it, and we shook solemnly.

"You ever change your mind about show business, we'll be back this way next year," I said.

"I don't think so," Fremont grunted, then grinned. "Maybe I'll sneak down and catch your act sometime."

"You do that, partner," I chuckled. But there was an ache in my chest that I knew wasn't caused by the altitude.

Fremont opened his other paw, and it was only then that I saw he'd been carrying something all this way. Very gently he put it on my head and slid the elastic under my chin.

His spangled hat.

"For you," Fremont said softly. "Something to remember me by. Maybe it will bring you luck."

"Maybe it already has," I managed to say.

Rita was shifting nervously from one foot to the other. Her eyes darted all around as the night sounds got louder. "I hate to spoil the moment, guys, but I think it's time for us nonnatives to beat it."

Fremont scooped Rita and I into a loving bear hug that left us gasping for air. "I don't know how to thank you . . . ," he began.

"Don't," I cut in. "Just run along, like a good bear." He set us down. "And don't take any wooden picnic baskets."

I turned away, and Rita and I started down the hill. Looking back, I saw the larger than life shape of my big buddy, darker than the shadows. He rose up on his hind legs to give us a last good-bye wave. Then he dropped to all fours and vanished into the forest.

Rita and I were quiet as we walked, each of us alone with our thoughts. It wasn't until we hit the out-

skirts of town that she spoke. And it wasn't in her usual jeering screech.

"I've been thinking, Pete. With Fremont out of the picture, you're gonna be looking for a new partner. I know we've had our little differences in the past—"

"Differences?" I snorted. "You mean, like you jerking my tail every chance you get? And making that 'in dog years you're dead' crack? And—"

"Oh, jeez, isn't that just like a dog, digging up every little bone to pick—"

She stopped herself, took a deep breath. "What I was going to say was maybe you and I could partner up. Come up with an act."

"Us? An act?" I asked. Actually, it sounded like a pretty good idea. But she didn't need to know that— yet. "You'd have to stop calling me Bone Breath," I warned. "Your mouth doesn't exactly smell like a bowl of roses either, you know."

"Done," she agreed.

"Right. And I get top billing. Pete and Rita."

"What happened to ladies first?" she asked.

"What lady?" I snapped.

"Rita and Pete! It sounds better!"

"Pete and Rita—or no dice."

Rita's eyes flashed. "Now listen here, Bone Breath—"

"Ha!"

Well, the rest you know. The minute word went around the tent that Fremont, Rita, and I had gotten safely away, the other animals went back to acting like professionals. Nobody was hurt, of course. Except Boston Charlie, who woke up ranting about how we'd plotted the whole thing to free the bear and shot him in the butt when he tried to stop us! Can you imagine?

The ringmaster sent Charlie to a place where he could have a long, long rest away from animals. We've got a nice young blond kid named Gunther Gumball-something working the big cats now.

Do I miss Fremont? Sure, sometimes. Whenever I see big mountains off in the distance or when a lightning storm wakes me up at night. And I know he misses me. But I'm never sorry that I helped him get home. I'm happy because I know he's happy.

That's how it is with friends.

I've still got that hat, of course. Wouldn't part with it for the world. A genuine lucky hat is hard to come by.

And guess what? Rita and I stopped snapping at each other long enough to work up an act that's headlined Circus Martinez ever since. The Stupendous, Colossal, and Amazing Pete and Rita. Don't tell her I said so, but the chimp's got talent.

Of course, she needed the right partner.

You've seen our poster, right? Tell you what, I'll leave you a couple of free tickets at the box office. Tell 'em Pete sent you.

Hey, have a piece of this pink popcorn. It's my favorite.